One Arctic Summer

Dani Haviland

USA Today Bestselling Author

One Arctic Summer is a work of fiction. Names, place, characters, and incidents are the product of the author's imagination and are used for the readers' enjoyment. Any resemblance to persons living, dead, or fictional, events or business establishments is entirely coincidental.

Book Description

Was she his Red Raven or just another cheechako, a tenderfoot from the outside world looking for excitement or a news story in his remote Alaskan village?

Embrace the trials, frustrations, and richness of life in Barrow (Utqiaġvik), Alaska with the local 'healer' who changed east coast archaeology intern Alexandra Oppenheimer's philosophy on life in 1994. Twenty-two years later, will the area be the same for her? And will Rocky have returned to it?

Acknowledgment

Thanks to the readers who suggest names when I can't quite put my finger on one. I was using X as a place saver when Jennifer Walz Rieth suggested the name Alexandra (or Bones). Alexandra stayed as the given name but having X as a defiant woman's nickname felt right, too.

Note

I visited Barrow (now called Utqiaġvik) in 1994, the same summer this story takes place. The scenery—including the archaeological dig—people and warmth I experienced in this area was the inspiration for my tale of second chance love.

Chapter 1

June 18th, 2016
Utqiaġvik (Barrow), Alaska

"The beach hasn't changed. Still the same tiny pebbles instead of sand or shells, Arctic milky-gray instead of tropical crystal-clear blue or Resurrection Bay green. When I left, this place was alive, vibrant—full of food for generations to come, the spirits of the water calling to those on shore, beckoning for man to come find the whales that were ready to cede their lives to feed the families of the two-legged souls who had chosen to leave the water-world and remain on the solid part of the earth."

"It's still full of food," Krista said. "True, the water has been eating away at the shore and the sea ice is melting, but there are still lots of fish in the water and seals and polar bears chasing after them. At least, that's what the text books and media claim."

Alexandra shook her head, sniffed and wiped her wind-chilled nose. "Yes, dear. That might be true, but it's not magical without him." She walked back up the rise with her daughter to the cordoned-off excavation site. She remembered it as being much further inland, but that was when global warming was just a forecast, not a reality. The seas had risen, the coastline eaten up by the rising waters, and the bluff was now almost at sea level.

"What's going on, Mom? And why do you look so dreamy-eyed? You're usually so analytical and reserved. Is there something wrong? Did you forget to pack your magnifying glass and hand sanitizer?" Krista joked and patted her on the shoulder. "If I had a mirror, I'd make you look in it. Honestly, Mom, you don't even look like you."

"Knock it off, Krista," Lars told his older sister. "I think she looks pretty. Mom, don't listen to her. I think you still, and always will, look like you. It's just that now you look like a prettier, happier you."

The mother laughed and shook her head, knocking off some of the dreaminess but letting the sweetness of her memories cling to her neck and shoulders, comforting her now that the cares of the world were beyond her reach.

"Come on, kids, let's head back toward the hotel.

There's a squall coming in and I don't care to get wet."

"How do you know?" Lars asked.

"The drop in the air pressure told me. If you're sensitive to it, you can actually feel the difference on your face."

"Huh?"

"Other than your eyes, the skin on your face is the most sensitive part of your body. Feel the air now, and when the rains come closer, we'll come back outside and see if you can tell."

"You're right, Krista. Mom's acting weird," Lars said, then ran ahead of the women, looking for something interesting in this barren land that his mother insisted was bountiful.

"Grandma Lou always said you grew up that summer," Krista said, "that you left Boston a spoiled and entitled brat but came back sweet, humble, and generous. What happened?"

"I met your father."

"No," Krista said and frowned, shaking her head. "Daddy said he'd never been to Alaska and never wanted anything to do with it."

"No, I met your father, not your daddy, God rest his soul."

She shrugged her shoulder and frowned with self-admonishment, letting the words sink in for her daughter. Krista's eyes widened in shock and her mouth dropped open, but words wouldn't come forth. She was a love child?

"I never gave your father the chance to be a daddy. I should have. Not that it made me care any less for the man I married and who gave you his last name and reared you as his own. You see, I met your daddy when you were eight months old, just before Christmas. Well, I think he fell in love with you first and then me, but it really doesn't matter. We had twenty wonderful years together. He's gone, and you're right, he said he'd never come to Alaska. I always wanted to come back, but I think he didn't want me to because he was afraid I'd meet the man who sired you. That dreamy look you accused me of? Well, I guess I got it whenever anyone mentioned Alaska. He knew who I was thinking about. It's not as if I would have ever cheated on him, but he was jealous of the love I shared with this other man. Ours was the kind of love that only comes once in a lifetime…"

"Mo-om," Lars said, "Do you have to talk all mushy like that when I'm around? Can't you wait until I find something else to do? Right now, I'm cold. Can I go in and play a video

4

game?"

"Nope."

"Why not?"

"Because it isn't here."

"But I packed it, Mom. I made sure I had the charger and everything."

"Yes, and I took it out of your backpack and threw in a couple extra pairs of clean socks. They'll serve you better than those little electronic blips eating each other."

"But there's nothing to do…"

"Take a walk. Explore the town. See how other people live, talk to them, see if you can find a pick-up basketball game."

"Aren't you afraid someone's going to kidnap me?" Lars asked, then swatted at the mosquito on his neck.

"Nope. What would they do if they stole you? Ask for ransom? Don't worry about the people here. It's not like you were in Boston or any other big city."

"Mom," Krista interjected, knowing that Lars could argue for hours about any topic, and it was better to cut him off before he got too wound up, "If Daddy wasn't my father, who was?"

"Okay," Lars said, "I have one question and then I'm outta here to go explore. Was Daddy my father?"

"Yup!" Alexandra said, her grin of satisfaction unmistakable. "It took seven years of doctors' visits, thousands and thousands of dollars in, shall we say, 'medical procedures,' and then I had you. You're my $30,000 baby."

"Cool! That's just as good as being a love child," Lars said, then darted away before his sister could slap him. "I'll be back before dark!"

"You be back to the hotel when you get hungry or by eight o'clock, whichever comes first. It won't get dark for another month!"

"So, Mom, why didn't you ever tell me?" Krista asked when they were alone.

"I could say it's complicated, but it was only because I didn't want to upset Daddy. Now that he's gone, it's time."

"So, did my father work up here with you on the dig? Was he an archeologist, too?" Krista shook her head. "He couldn't have been because I have no interest whatsoever in dry bones. Now, if he was a musician or a doctor, that I could understand."

Alexandra didn't even try to keep the sly smile from her

face. She'd answer one question at a time and reveal the whole story over the next few days. Ever since high school, it was rare that her daughter engaged her in conversation. She'd take all the time with her she could.

"No, he wasn't an archeologist, but he did help me on the dig. Do you want to hear the whole story? I mean, except for the personal parts."

"Ew! I certainly don't want to hear how I was conceived! Yes, please stick to the PG and PG-13 rated parts."

"I was twenty-one and fresh out of Tufts University…"

Chapter 2

Twenty-two years earlier
June 18, 1994
Barrow (Utqiaġvik), Alaska

Ding! Ding!

The grim-faced young woman in designer jeans and a high-dollar rain jacket buttoned up to her chin smacked the chrome-bell on the counter, then craned her neck and looked down the short hall for the attendant.

Frustration raised her voice an octave higher as she called out toward the back of the small convenience market, "Hey! Is anyone working here?"

"He's unloading the truck," a male voice said softly, his choppy meter indicating he was native to the area.

Alexandra jumped at the sound. "Oh! I didn't see you there. Do you know if they have any cocoa butter moisturizing cream here? I brought a big bottle of it with me, but the airport security took it out of my carryon. As if hand lotion could be used to make a bomb!"

8

"You never know," the twenty-something year old Native man said dryly, then brought the small packet of paper he held close to his face, inspecting it. Holding the rolling paper and herbs in one hand, he used the point of his pencil to push a wayward strand of leafy material down, then licked one edge of the paper and rolled a perfect cigarette.

"Smoking's a disgusting habit," she said, then brushed her auburn hair behind her ear and walked away to the opposite side of the three-aisle store to inspect the limited supply of cans on the shelf.

Rocky chuckled softly and set the rolled 'cigarette' of his custom blend of herbs and dried seaweed next to the others on the plate near the window.

Alexandra turned sharply at his laugh and snapped back, "Well, it is!"

"So is judging others on outward appearances," he said.

Just then, Q walked in from the back of the store, wiping his hands on a red handkerchief that he stuffed back into his hip pocket. "Not much came in today, but maybe next week will be better. Hey, there," he said as he nodded toward the plate in the window next to his cousin. "Looks like you got quite a bunch of those rolled for Margaret. I don't know what to say but thanks, Rocky. I never thought anything would relieve her asthma. All the inhalers and pills they give her at the Native hospital did nothing but bloat her face and make her want to eat all the time. I'm not sure what you put in these but smoking one of them every once in a while sure opens up her airways. What do I owe you?"

"Same as always, Q. Dinner one of these nights and…"

Alexandra interrupted the two men, waving a can of chili in the air. "Are you kidding me? Five bucks for a can of chili? You have to be out of your ever-lovin' mind!"

Q and Rocky looked at each other, their grins identical, their dark eyes dancing as they silently decided who was going to be the one to give this cheechako the lecture on the costs involved with bringing 'Outside' food into Barrow. Just as Q was ready to explain the economics behind his pricing, the base station radio crackled.

"Hey, Q. It's me, Big Ben. We got another one. Over."

"Roger that. Rocky's here with me now. What's your location and situation?"

"Half mile before you get to the polar bear sign. Make sure Rocky has lots of cat gut. Little Ben was showing off. The cut's not deep, but it is long."

Rocky reached beside the duct tape-patched kitchen chair he sat in and grabbed what looked like a plastic tackle box. He held it up for Q to see, then stood up and grabbed the hand-held radio from the charger.

"We're on our way. Over and out," Q said, then let his finger off the radio switch, following Rocky out the door before it shut.

Alexandra set the chili back on the shelf and raced outside, shouting after the pair, "So, does this mean I have to wait before I can buy anything?"

Q stuck his fist out the truck window and gave her a thumb's up, then grabbed the steering wheel and shifted gears. Little Ben was big for an Inupiaq, but he was also diabetic. Even a minor wound could cause major problems. Rocky and Q didn't have time for a prissy white woman and neither did Little Ben.

***

"Well, it's about time!" X groused when the two men came in an hour and a half later. "What'd you do? Stop off for a beer?"

Q and Rocky shared that same brown-eyed twinkle of 'should I tell her, or do you want to?' This time, Rocky shrugged a shoulder to Q, accepting the task.

"Barrow is a damp town. There's no place—bars or taverns—for us to drop in and have a beer. Besides, neither of us drink." He looked around and saw the displays had been dusted and the cans and boxes straightened and brought forward so the shelves looked fuller than they actually were. "Thanks for sprucing up the place. Did you decide what you wanted?"

Alexandra huffed then slid the can of chili and a can of evaporated milk toward the vintage cash register. "Do you happen to have a can opener and a microwave here? I can use my pocketknife to punch a hole in the canned milk for my tea in the morning, but it won't work for the chili."

"Microwave's right over there and the can opener is right next to it," Rocky said.

"You pay me," Q said. "I'm the owner. He just hangs out here."

"Hmph," she remarked with one eyebrow raised, then took a twenty-dollar bill out of her Gucci shoulder bag and handed it to him. "And make sure you count back the change; don't just dump it in my hand."

"Yes, ma'am," Q said, fighting back a full-blown laugh at

her rudeness.

"I'm a miss!" she said, flipping her hair back.

"Yes, miss!" Q replied, fighting back the urge to salute her. Instead, he stuck his hands in the till and took out the change. "Ten, fifteen, twenty dollars. Thank you for your business, *miss*. Have a nice day."

"Hmph!"

Alexandra grabbed her high-priced cans and strutted to the microwave next to the hallway. Grabbing the can opener with an exaggerated flourish, she spread its jaws and clamped down on the lid, squeezing the handle and twisting the knob with a vengeance. Once the lid was canted up, she held it by the edges and neatly dropped it into the waste basket next to the counter. It was then that she realized she didn't have a bowl to put it into or a spoon to remove the contents.

"You can buy some paper plates or bowls," Q offered, "or dump it into a coffee cup. I usually don't let folks have a cup without buying coffee, but since you're new around here, you can use the cup for free." He reached under the counter and brought out a single porcelain cup, coffee-stained brown, the handle chipped but usable.

"Thanks," she said, scowling at the marginally sanitary vessel. "How about a spoon? Is there a charge for that?"

"Not unless you take it outside the store." Q took the spoon from beside the coffee pot that held an inch of overcooked java and wiped it with the red handkerchief from his back pocket. "Don't forget to give it back when you're done."

"Yeah, it's part of a set," Rocky added with a chuckle, then went back to rolling the rest of the herbal blend in his mis-matched plastic container.

Alexandra took the spoon hesitantly, her stomach growling to hurry up and get it done. With her back to the men, she reached in her purse and removed a tissue from its small packet and re-wiped the spoon. She turned back and dumped half the food into the cup, covering the contents with the tissue so the chili didn't splatter all over the inside of the microwave. When she opened the oven door, she gasped. "Oh, my goodness! When was the last time someone cleaned this?"

"Was it my turn this year?" Rocky quipped. "Or maybe that was last year, and I forgot..."

"Ergh! I guess it'll have to do. At least with the tissue on top, the old baked-on crud won't fall into it!"

Alexandra pushed the set-time and start buttons, but nothing happened. She pushed the quick cook for popcorn and nothing happened with that, either. "How do you get this thing to work?"

"Oh," Q said with as straight a face as he could manage. "I told you we have a microwave. You never asked if it worked or not."

"Now how am I supposed to eat this?" she screeched, waving the spoon in the air.

"With the spoon would probably be the least messy way," Rocky said, then licked the paper on the last herbal smoke, looking down at his project to keep from laughing out loud.

"But it's cold!"

"Yeah, and once it's in your belly, it'll be warm," Q said. "What's the problem? At least it's not frozen. If it was, it might break your teeth."

"Ergh!" Alexandra growled again, this time adding a hiking boot foot stomp for emphasis.

"You know, if you're not going to eat that, I'll need my cup and spoon back," Q said. "If you don't want it, my dog will get rid of it for you. He's more of a fish-eater, but he's been known to chow down on Mexican beef and chilis. The folks over at Pepe's save their scraps for us who have dogs."

"What's Pepe's?" she asked as she inspected the reddish-brown blob on her spoon.

"The Mexican restaurant at Cape Smythe. You don't have much choice for cheechako food up here. It's pretty much either Mexican or pizza. Oh, and I wouldn't expect much in the way of salad or fresh fruits and vegetables if that's what you're looking for."

Alexandra's stomach roared again. It knew that even if she went somewhere else to eat, it would be at least an hour before she actually got to consuming the food off the end of a fork. "When in Rome," she grumbled, and stabbed the spoon in the cup. She pulled out a lump of brown gravy-covered meat and took a bite. Chewing slowly, she realized it wasn't as bad as she had feared.

"Would you like some chips with your chili?" Q asked, waving a small snack-sized bag of corn chips. "Only two bucks a bag."

She swallowed the bite in her mouth before answering, her taste buds eager for a flavor other than straight red chili.

"Are there any hidden costs?" she asked, setting the cup on the counter to get into her purse.

"Nope. I'll even throw in a paper napkin since you're a repeat customer."

"Deal!" she said, handing him two one-dollar bills.

She pulled on the sides of the bag, trying to open in, then tugged harder, the bag exploding and scattering its contents all over the floor.

"Shit! Shit! Shit!"

Rocky set down his empty herb container and ran to her side, stopping short of touching her. "Don't worry. Today's your lucky day. It's not often we have a money-back guarantee. Q, get me another bag."

"Ahem…"

"It's covered by the dinner you owe me," Rocky said, and grabbed the chips from Q's hand. He pulled the Leatherman tool out of his front pocket and slit the top open.

"Here," he said and offered it to her. "Sometimes it's safer to use a knife. Or at least, there's less food wasted."

"I'll take care of the mess," Q said. He walked to the back door. "Come on in, Fish Face," he called to his dog. "I got another floor cleaning job for you."

Alexandra looked around the store again. Other than the stool behind the cash register and the old kitchen chair her knife-toting new acquaintance had been in, there was no place to sit.

Rocky saw the search for a seat and took the lead. "Here, let me get my stuff out of the way. You can set your cup in the window while you eat your chips. You might want to buy a bottle of water or soda, too. There aren't any drinking fountains around here."

Her resolve to stay strong in the strange new land was wearing thin. Between delayed flights, lost luggage and the hotel reservation that the university had never made, Alexandra was spent—depleted and depressed and without a place to stay for the night. Her head shook back and forth slowly as she made her way to the duct-taped chair.

"Are you going to be all right?" Rocky asked.

"I don't know," she said, sniffing back the tears. "I thought it was because I was so hungry. I haven't eaten anything for," she looked at her watch. "What day is it?"

"Saturday," Rocky said and crossed his arms across his chest, stuffing his hands under his armpits, making sure he didn't reach out to comfort her.

"Crap!"

Q and Rocky looked at her but didn't say a word.

"Well, at least I didn't say 'shit.'"

Both men nodded minimally in agreement.

"You save that for spilled food, I guess," Rocky said, and winked at her.

Alexandra's mouth twitched as she tried to contain her smile. She had worked so hard for her degree, to get those letters after her name so she'd be respected, and now what happens? She melts down in front of a couple of locals who probably don't own a spare shirt between the two of them.

"What's the matter?" Rocky prompted, watching her waver between letting her human side out and continuing with the proper and uptight college snob facade. "Did you lose a day, your job, luggage, resolve..."

"Yes, I did. Or at least, most of the above. That idiot at the university didn't make my hotel reservation, I guess. At least, they can't find it. I thought today was Friday and I could call and get the name they reserved the room under, but that isn't going to happen since today's tomorrow and no one is in the offices on the weekend. Yes, on the luggage, too. The airlines told me to check back tomorrow. That is, if the plane comes in. They said something about scheduled maintenance or something. My job? I'm an intern. I don't get paid. I'm slave labor, working for the experience. I need a certain number of hours in the field before they'll even consider me for an appointment where I want to be. Resolve…"

Alexandra took a big bite of the chili, then shoved three chips in her mouth and chewed thoroughly, wishing she had something to wash it down with. Since she was scraping by on what was in her wallet, she worked up some spit and swallowed. "I'm tougher than I look."

"Well, I don't know…" Q said. "You got mighty upset about spilled chips…"

"I think you look very tough," Rocky said, turning his flirtatious wink into a blink hidden by a feigned cough. "You're probably thousands of miles from home, no place to stay, limited funds, eating canned chili and chips in a convenience store at the northernmost city in America…"

Alexandra dropped the spoon before it got to her mouth, spilling its contents down the front of her raincoat. "Shit! Yes, right now my life sucks! Thanks for spelling it out for me!"

Rocky grabbed the handkerchief out of Q's hip pocket

and made a hasty clean-up of the chili on the front of her clothes, backing off on wiping up the smaller smears left behind. He stood back, shook out the contents on the floor, called, "Fish Face, food!" and stood back.

The three-legged black dog came running from the back of the store and quickly licked up all traces of the spill.

"I can fix you up with a place to stay for the night," Rocky said. "No charge. As far as everything else, I'm sure it'll work out."

She looked up and saw he was serious—a genuinely concerned person. It didn't matter whether he was male or female, young or old, all she saw was sincerity and willingness to help a fellow human being in distress. Try finding that at an east coast university!

"All right. I appreciate it. I sure hope you have something to drink, though."

Rocky nodded, then reached into the nook by the window and took his herbal storage container. "Are you ready?"

Alexandra's mouth opened, ready to say yes, when she held up a finger. "Just a sec. Hey, Fish Face. Food!"

The dog came lumbering back out, not as hungry now

that he'd had chips and a bit of dip.

"How about a little spot-cleaning," she said, then squatted down and stuck her chest out so the dog could lick off the remains of the chili.

'My kind of woman,' went through Rocky's head. He looked over at Q and saw the same look of appreciation on his cousin's face. He shook his head minimally, reminding him that he was married.

Q scowled at him. 'Yeah, I know, I know...'

She stood back up, then reached into the window sill for the cup of chili, chips, and the spoon. "Oh, and here you go," and handed the chili cup and spoon to Q. "I might need these for breakfast," holding up the chips, "just in case things don't work out."

"Ready?" Rocky asked again, holding open the door.

"Resolve returned. Yes, I'm ready."

When they were outside, Alexandra looked around. "Where's your truck?"

"I don't own a truck. That was Q's. Oh, and I'm Rocky, by the way."

"Rocky By-the-way? That's a funny last name. What's it short for?"

"How about you tell me what they call you and then I'll explain the etymology of my name."

"Whoa! Big word for such a small-town boy."

"All right, Whoa Big-word…" Rocky mocked, his left eye squinted as he peered into her face, letting her know she had just insulted him.

"Oh, I'm sorry, I'm sorry. That was rude. It's just they advised us in school to use smaller words in smaller communities, especially in remote areas with limited access to communications and libraries and… Please accept my apology."

Rocky shrugged one shoulder. She wasn't the first college snob who'd come into this town. Researchers came and left, looking for the next big find or news story, whether it be whales stuck in the ice or thousand-year-old mummies preserved in the permafrost. They were all the same—transients. Snobs who slung around big words, trying to impress others while they sought the meaning of life. They'd stick around for a few weeks, then hustle back to the cluttered and putrid existences they had come from. He'd stay where he was, where the traditions of his ancestors fed both the bodies and the souls of those who stayed around to be nurtured.

"My name is Alexandra Oppenheimer, but I go by X."

"Makes signing your name much easier, I'm sure," Rocky said, adding a wink.

"Just don't call me X-rated. I hate it when people say that."

Rocky's eyes widened in shock. "I'd never suggest…" he said, then closed his mouth before he did say something embarrassing.

"You're blushing, Rocky! I don't think I've ever seen a grown man blush before."

Rocky took a deep breath, started to offer an excuse, then decided it was best to play the small-town dunce. She'd be gone in a day or two anyhow. Why waste words on the wind, the sparkle of emotion she tickled out of him wouldn't be returned or appreciated. She was a fleshy package but probably had little, if any, substance. She was merely a shadow of the person he had seen in his dreams. His red-haired raven—the other half of his soul—was just that: a dream.

"Well?" she asked. "I don't know where we're going, and I'm sorry if I sound rude, but I'm not used to this cold. Does the sun ever come out around here?"

"This way," he said, and pointed past the airport. "And the sun *is* out and won't go down until August first. It's just cloudy. Come November, you won't see the sun for two months. But don't worry, I have it on good authority that it'll return by late January. Happens every year like clockwork."

"You mean like calendar-work?"

"Nope. I don't think there is even such a word, Miss. Like clockwork on the clock of the grand scale of life, not the itty bitty electronic or geared mechanisms of man," Rocky said, giving her a weak, half-hearted smile.

"What did I do to piss you off? Dang, you're moodier than I am!"

Rocky ignored her question. She wouldn't understand his disappointment at another red head coming into his life who wasn't the right one. "Where we're going is just down the road. I live with my grandmother. I sleep on the couch in the living room. There's only one bedroom in the house and she sleeps in it. I think I'd better warn you, though. If she offers to share her bed with you, I suggest you decline. The bed's comfortable enough, and she doesn't snore, but she tosses and turns and kicks and…" He shook his head. "She doesn't

25

do it on purpose," he said, then smiled his sly grin, "At least, I don't think so. You can have the couch and I'll take the floor until you get your housing situation settled."

X opened her mouth to protest, and a burp sneaked out. "Oops! Excuse me."

"Canned chili. It'll do it every time," Rocky said, then pointed to the small unpainted house. "We're here."

Chapter 3

"Thanks for letting me stay with your family. It really does mean a lot to me. I don't think this level of hospitality would be shown you if you were stranded in my hometown."

X saw the shadow of a frown creep up on Rocky's face and realized that her remark sounded prejudiced against Natives. "Shown you or me or anyone else—young or old, for that matter."

Rocky chuckled at her uneasiness. "Disrespect doesn't care about gender, age, or ethnicity. Generous and rude people are as diverse as the rocks on the earth."

"Hey, I like that. Some are as tough as obsidian or diamonds, others as flaky as mica."

Rocky grinned at her appreciation of his colorful and unusual analogy. "And some are as precious as gold or gems, some as worthless as the mud on the bottom of a boot."

X added, "Old as the hills or new as spewed lava. Gee, Rocky, we could go on all night."

His chest rose and fell in a silent laugh, keeping back the

type of comments he and Q usually tossed back and forth when the women weren't around. Ever since Q had married, their time together had evaporated, their evening chit chats and commentaries on everything from who was running for mayor to what was the best motor to have on a whaling boat had dried up. He wouldn't have to worry about that for long now, though. A little more than two weeks and it would be time for him to leave.

"I said, did you know the difference between magma and lava?" X asked, apparently not for the first time.

"I'm sorry. I was distracted by a random thought... Yes, I know the difference. Do you?"

X took a deep breath, ready to defend her intelligence, to remind him in her brash eastern manner that she was a college graduate with a minor in geology... Then she relaxed, foregoing the complicated spiel she would have given the bar patrons she served at the tavern near the university. She didn't need to protect her self-esteem with a synthetic thick skin in this village. These were real people.

She shrugged a shoulder. "Lava is simply magma—that is, molten rock—that has left the earth's crust."

"Yeah, that's what I heard, too. Some rocks just can't

take the heat…"

"Or they want to go to the beach…" X added. "Hey, speaking of the beach, do you think you could show me where the dig site is? I have a map in here somewhere…" She opened her backpack and pawed fruitlessly through the contents until he spoke.

"We don't need a map. It's just down the road. Everyone knows where it is. My grandmother said that is where her ancestors lived. Her family has been in this neighborhood since before walrus had whiskers."

"Does that mean you plan on living here until you have grandchildren?"

Rocky leaned forward, as if to tell her a secret, then whispered, "I have to have children first. And in order to have children, I have to be married." He stood up and resumed speaking in his usual soft voice, "And in order to be married, I have to find the right woman. I know just about everyone in this village and… Scratch that. I *do know* everyone in this village, and she's not here."

"You don't know me," X said, then realized that by being literally correct, she was making a pass. "I mean…I mean…you know my name, and a little about me, but I'm sure there are others in this town you don't know."

"Nope. The only one I don't know is you and anyone else who just stepped off the plane and is staying at the hotel. Logistically, only half would be women, and of those, half of them would be married. And of those, all of them will be leaving before winter." *And I'll be gone before then!*

"So, can we go see the dig site now or do we have to wait until morning?" X asked, eager to change the subject.

"Why wait? It's plenty light now. Unless you want a little muktuk."

"What's that?"

"Dinner."

"I mean, what is it in words I'd relate to?"

"Whale skin with a chunk of blubber attached to it. Got a nutty flavor to it, or so I've heard. It just tastes like muktuk to me."

"No, thanks. I think I'll pass. That chili didn't sit too well. Whale blubber for dessert might just tip the scales in the wrong direction."

The two walked toward the beach down the unpaved road, side by side, a cautious two feet away from each other. Rocky noticed a former classmate and his girlfriend walking toward him, hand-in-hand, their smiles identical.

"Hey, there, Oscar, Lisa. Anything but mosquitoes biting down there?"

Oscar slipped him a sly smile and a wink. "Nothing that I care to talk about. We weren't fishing. Just taking a walk."

Lisa leaned in close to Oscar and kissed him quick on the cheek, then pulled back and hugged his elbow close to her. "Tell him. It's okay. He's our friend."

"We're going to have a baby," he said. "Oh, and we're going to get married, too."

"Babies can come anytime," Rocky said. "Weddings are generally planned."

All four of them laughed, then Lisa gently tugged at her fiancé's arm. "Let's go. It's getting too windy."

Oscar rolled his eyes. He knew what she wanted. More alone time. Her parents were out of town and they had the house to themselves in the afternoon while her brother was at work. "Just a sec." He turned to Rocky and asked, "So, did you find your red raven?" nodding toward X.

"Huh? Oh, no. This is Alexandra Oppenheimer. She's the intern for the archaeologist at the new dig site. She's only here for the rest of the summer," Rocky said, then added a

31

sideways glance that Oscar and Lisa understood to mean, 'If she lasts that long.'

"Welcome to Utqiaġvik," Oscar said.

X's eyes looked from Rocky back to Oscar. "I thought this was Barrow…"

"Maybe to you it's Barrow, but to us who have been in the area for generations, it's Utqiaġvik, the place to hunt snowy owls. Or get potatoes, depending on who's version of site names you're reading. To us, it's just home."

"Well, either way, it's a wonderful warm town, despite the wind. Nice meeting both of you. Or would that be all three of you?" X asked.

Lisa giggled behind her hand. "Nice to meet you, too," she said, then led Oscar away, whispering to her fiancé, "I like her. I think Rocky likes her, too. He just doesn't know it yet."

Seeing the couple walk away awoke something in X. She wasn't sure what it was, but suddenly, she had the biggest urge to mimic Lisa and cuddle into Rocky's side. "Lisa was right, there is a chilly wind blowing," she said, using the line as her excuse to stand nearer and share his warmth.

Rocky brought up his arm and wrapped it around her

shoulder, bringing her close with two quick and gentle tugs toward him, reassuring her that it was okay, she wasn't being too forward. Suddenly, this felt so right, holding her. Maybe she really was his red raven and his spirit soulmate had just been playing the trickster.

A few minutes later they arrived at the site, white cording partitioning off the area from the rest of the grassy bluff above the beach.

"Not much to look at from here," she said, and burrowed deeper into him.

Rocky pulled her jacket collar up, leaning into her hair as he did so, inhaling her spicy scent, her unbound auburn hair flying about, tickling his nose. "Make sure you bundle up when you come to work. If your luggage doesn't get here in time, we'll figure something out. You won't be thinking clearly if you're shivering from the cold. Plus, your hands will be stiff and won't work."

"I don't have to come here tomorrow. From the tentative schedule that was set up before I left, I'm supposed to show up at the dig on Monday morning. Dr. J. said first light, but I'm pretty sure he was messing with me since he knew about the twenty-four hours of daylight at this time of year. After he said that, he added, 'Or eight o'clock, whichever suits you.'"

X squatted down and peered into the area that had already been partially excavated. She looked up at Rocky. "We call the man, pardon my speech, Dr. Jackass. He was a newly tenured associate professor until the head of the department keeled over from a heart attack. Next thing you know, Dr. J.'s in charge of all the American archaeological digs. He always wanted to come to Alaska, but he wasn't in line for it. He made a few calls and suddenly he was top dog on the dig, even though Dr. Peterson had been on the schedule to come up here for over a year. Men!"

"What brought that on?" Rocky asked, and squatted down beside her, enjoying her nearness despite her exasperation.

"Dr. Peterson is a woman. She's as smart as they come but there's the matter of tenure. She started on her doctorate late in life because she wanted to have children before she was too old. Beautiful kids, too. Anyhow, even though she was slated to come up here, he bumped her off the schedule and took her place. He couldn't add her as an assistant because then they'd have to pay her and that wasn't in the budget. That position was for an unpaid intern. I wasn't supposed to come out either. Scotty was next in line for the internship, but I guess Dr. J. liked my body-type more and asked for me by name. As if I'd ever let that sexist, ego-bloated…"

X looked over and saw Rocky's eyes widen, shock ready to take over if she continued her rant. "I'm sorry. He has, shall we say, tried to take liberties with me. I may be single, but he's a married man. Even if we were both single, unsolicited advances are unwelcome."

Rocky patted her shoulder, then stood up. "Come on. The wind is getting stronger as the sun gets lower. Let's get back to my grandmother's house."

***

"Grandmother, this is Alexandra. Both her luggage and her hotel reservation were lost. I've invited her to stay with us for the night."

Grandma looked X up and down, the lack of eye contact with her guest indicating she didn't need to include her in the conversation. "She can sleep with me," she said to Rocky.

"No, grandmother. She and I already discussed it."

Rocky looked over at X and fixed her with a 'don't challenge me on this—I know her, and you don't' stare. "I can sleep on the floor and she'll take the couch."

"No. She can sleep with me," Grandma said, punctuating her declaration with a stomp of her cane on the wooden floor.

X opened her mouth, ready to agree with her simply to end the tension but balked when she caught Rocky's glare. She closed her mouth quickly, and a forced smile took its place.

"Grandma, she's not used to this house. If she's a sleepwalker, then she'll step on me before going outside. We wouldn't want our guest to wake up in the lagoon now, would we?"

"Hmph! No. She stay on the couch and you sleep on the floor. You two come to bingo with me in one hour. She can help me mark my cards. My eyes not so good anymore. She has young, pretty eyes. I like her. She has red hair, too. Just like your great-great-grandfather."

She looked at X, speaking to her for the first time. "He's part Russian, you know," nodding to Rocky. "No red hair in family since me, but now mine's all white. Maybe he'll have red-haired children if he finds the right wife." She nodded thoughtfully. "I think Wilma in Wainwright has red-haired granddaughter. I'll ask her how old she is. I need to see great-grandchildren before I die. I want at least one with red hair like me."

Grandma finished her dissertation on the search for a redheaded wife for her grandson, then toddled over to her rocking chair, picking up her bag of yarn before she sat down. "Maybe she will have a little girl and name her Krista like me." She picked out her work in process—a soft brown scarf—and began crocheting, pacing her rocking with her hook work. "That would be nice. Very nice."

Rocky canted his head toward the kitchen, his eyes asking X to meet him there. This latest match with Grandma had ended in a tie. He had won the sleeping assignments, but she had someone to escort her to bingo.

"Is she always that insistent?"

"Yup, she's a redhead. Actually, I don't think hair color has anything to do with it. Elders pretty much get their way with everything. After all, they have had a lifetime of experience to learn from. I know in *modern* society, it's not that way. But in older cultures, we understand that unless there's some sort of impairment, the old folks generally know what's going on. 'Been there, done that' is real for them."

X shrugged her shoulder in a non-committal fashion. The only older people she was familiar with were aloof professors. She didn't care about their attitude and biased opinions, and the few times she had reached out, they let her know they didn't care about hers, either. Instead of commenting, she asked, "Can I call the airport and see if my luggage made it in yet?"

Rocky stuck out his bottom lip and shook his head, then looked at the rack of handmade coats and kuspuks hanging on the hooks lining the plasterboard wall. The jackets were for him to mend, the kuspuks—women's cotton print overgarments—were torn or worn-out beyond favor from their previous owners and he was supposed to cut them into rags, reclaiming any large pieces of usable fabric for quilts or other projects. He sighed at the possibilities, then shook his head again in case she had missed it.

She hadn't. "Why not? Why can't I call the airport?"

"You could if you went to the neighbor's house and asked them very nicely if you could use their phone. We don't have one. Or you could walk two blocks and ask the agent yourself, but all you'd get out of that would be exercise. No more flights are coming in today. Unless the airlines had a special request from you to transfer your bag to the cargo company and that plane came in a day early, your luggage isn't here."

"So, now what am I supposed to do? Wear the same clothes for another day?"

Rocky looked at her and grinned. "They look clean enough to me. Even your coat got a quick semi-dry cleaning from Fish Face. But if it makes you feel better, I have an idea. You'll have to wear the same pants until I figure something else out, but I have some kuspuks here that are usable. I know this one is from a woman who is about the same size as you. All I need to do is mend a couple of rips. It may not be the prettiest, but you can wear it over your clothes to keep them clean."

X's frown of frustration quickly turned into a smirk of satisfaction. "If only my mother could see me now, getting ready to have a man dress me in a reclaimed and patched kuspuk while working for free in the semi-frozen tundra, hundreds of miles within the Arctic Circle. She'd turn twelve shades of purple. Yup, Rocky, whatever you can do to help me out is much appreciated. I'm still working on 'unlearning' the useless set of values my mother did her best to instill in me. I'm sure I'll survive without designer lotions and clothing."

"These are designer clothes, and if you need some lotion, I have something that I'm sure is just as good, if not better than, the cocoa cream butter you were looking for. Since I blended it from an old family recipe, it's designer, too."

"Design away! This may not be my home, but I feel more comfortable here, right now with you and your grandmother, than I have anywhere else since I summered with my own grandmother when I was eight."

"If that's the case, go in the living room and chat with Grandma for a bit while I get this finished. We have less than an hour until it's time for bingo."

Grandma regaled X with the stories of her youth, of the winter of near starvation when her husband had been injured after his crew had towed a big bowhead to the shore. The men were maneuvering the massive creature for butchering when the tow line snapped, the sheave block hitting her husband in the thigh bone, breaking his femur, the gaping wound and loss of blood threatening to take his life.

She had been on the beach that day, her young

daughter slung close to her body under her coat, ready to assist in the butchering. She told X how she had elbowed the men aside and took over the job of quickly setting the bone and holding his wound closed, staunching the flow of blood with her tight grasp. The men put her husband on the flat board that was supposed to be used as a processing table for the meat and carried him inside the church. She shuffled alongside him, her grasp on his thigh tight, the baby inside her coat squirming and squalling because she had been jostled from her nursing position. She ignored the infant's wails, knowing the baby could be late in a meal but her husband couldn't afford to lose another drop of blood.

Once inside, she directed her nephew to get her medical satchel and take out one of the needles she always kept on hand threaded with a suture, soaking in a bottle of vanilla extract. He pulled out the suture, handed her the needle, and took over her job holding his uncle's leg together.

She quickly flexed her hand, working the circulation back in her frozen and stiff fingers, then bent to work, stitching the muscle together first before finalizing her work by pulling his blue-tinged flesh together. The loss of blood was extreme. Only time would tell if her efforts were worth it or not.

The village did the best they could to help her with food and fuel that winter while he healed, but times were tough for them, too. With all the ado about taking him to the church for mending, the whale had washed back out to sea. It was more than a month before another whale was harvested, this one much smaller. Some said it was bad luck brought on by some of the people in the village drinking the white man's whisky and others said it was simply the circle of life—some years were prosperous, some were lean.

"We survived, but my husband was never the same. We lost our daughter, but that wasn't his fault. She was weak to start with, and because there wasn't enough food for me, I couldn't produce enough milk. He thought that if he had been more careful, he wouldn't have been hurt, they wouldn't have lost the whale, and his daughter wouldn't have perished. There was nothing I or anyone else could do to convince him that she wasn't ready for this world yet, that she was safe and sound in another world."

Grandma shrugged her shoulder. "I couldn't undo the past and neither could he. I decided to make the present and future a better place instead. I guess if I hadn't lost her, I wouldn't be so determined. She taught me a lesson and so did he."

"Did you ever have any more children?" X asked, enthralled with the story. "Of course, you did or you wouldn't have your grandson."

"Not with my husband. He left the next year. Then there was this one special man…" Grandma giggled. "I had a daughter by him—Rocky's mother. He left before I even knew I was pregnant. Rocky's mother and I had a challenging life, but we did okay. She stayed here until he was born. Then there was this one special man…" She grinned and waved her hand, letting X know that she had left with him, leaving Rocky with her.

X's eyes widened, then she swallowed her chagrin. Grandma had set her up on purpose and was waiting for her shocked reaction. Instead, X chuckled and said, "Yes, there's always that one special man…"

Grandma reached over and patted X on the leg. "I like you Alexandra. You remind me of me. You're a sharp woman. I don't think you found your special man yet, but you will. There's always that one man…" She drifted off into her own world of memories, picked up her crochet hook, and started back on the scarf. "Always that one special man you'll never forget..."

Rocky shook his head as he waited for a break in the story. "Ahem. Are you ready to try on your hand-me-down, custom-repaired designer kuspuk?" he asked, holding up the bright yellow calico overdress.

"Wow! That's beautiful." X felt the cotton fabric, worn soft from years of use and washing. "This feels better than any synthetic suede or polyester blend I've ever worn. How do I wear it?"

"Slip it over your head. The hood will keep your hair and the mosquitos out of your face, sort of."

X pulled the kuspuk over her head, then put her arms in the sleeves. "Uh, oh. The sleeves are too short."

"Nope. They're just right. Or they're going to have to be. There isn't enough fabric to make them longer. Besides, you don't want them dangling into your project."

"Good point. Are we ready to go?" X asked, noting that Grandma had left her rocker and was waiting by the door, holding onto her walking stick, swaying her hips to the music in her head, her joy evident in her smile of peace.

Rocky looked around the room, then took in a quick breath of 'aha' when he saw the bingo cards were still on the bookshelf. "We'll need these," he said, then grabbed the bundle of laminated cards. He walked over and opened the door for his grandmother. "After you, ladies."

Grandma lead the way, the confidence in her quick step setting the pace for the short two-block trip to the white-washed church. "Combination church, bingo parlor, and community hall in one. Oh, and voting center when needed."

"Where is everyone?" X asked, noting that only an older gentleman was in attendance. He was at a small table in the corner, bent over a project, a small engraving tool's black cord trailing over his hand as he worried the implement over a narrow, two-foot-long ivory-colored piece.

"They'll be here. I come early to set up. Let me introduce you to Joe. He's the heart of the community. Or something like that..." Rocky said, leading her to where the old man was seated, his Grandmother heading off in the other direction.

"Joe Williams, this is Alexandra Oppenheimer. She's here to..."

Joe put up his hand, stopping him politely. "I know. She's here to dig around in our ancestors' home. I already heard. I also heard you tell her I'm the heart of the community." Joe held up his carving, twisting the long, smooth and sturdy piece for her to see. "I'm really something else," he whispered to X. "Just ask the ladies."

Rocky blushed but held his tongue. Maybe Joe wouldn't embarrass him this time.

Nope.

"What is it?" X asked Joe, fingering the long smooth piece sporting fresh etchings at the base. "I've never seen anything so beautiful."

"It's an oosik," Joe said, his eyes twinkling at the opportunity to speak with the young and curious woman with flowing red hair.

"I'm sorry. I don't know what an oosik is? Is it part of a whale?"

"Nope. A whale doesn't have an oosik, and neither does a man, although some folks say that he used to have one, that it was called Adam's rib and that he gave to Eve." Joe chuckled, waiting for the line that was sure to come.

And there it was.

"So, what is an oosik?"

"A penis bone," Joe said, running his hand up and down the shaft slowly and seductively. "This one's from a narwhal. I'm giving it as a gift to my lady friend."

Grandma walked up and stabbed her walking stick just inches from old Joe's foot. "Are you playing with your penis bone again, Joe. I thought I asked you to stop embarrassing the ladies with that."

"You're just jealous because I won't give you my bone," he said, his eyes shining with a flirt.

X and Rocky stepped back from the interchange, both eager to be away from the elderly couple and their sexual innuendos.

"You'd give me your bone if I wanted it," Grandma said, "but it's been handled by so many, I'm afraid it'd give me a disease!"

"I could wash it…" Joe said, then set the oosik down on the table next to the engraver, "or I could let you clean it for me…" He kissed her gently on the cheek. "You going to let me tuck you into bed tonight, Krista?"

"No! I have a guest tonight," she said adamantly, then changed her tone and added a smile. "Maybe tomorrow night, though."

Suddenly, her smile was gone, and her business face was on. She turned away from Joe, looking for her grandson. "Did you get everything ready, Rocky?"

"Just waiting for you, Grandma."

Grandma Krista moved over to the long side of the banquet table, stomping her cane as she walked, changing her focus from a possible romantic fling with her randy friend to her real passion: music. She set her diamond willow walking stick against the wall and flexed her fingers in front of her face, bringing her elbows up with an exaggerated flourish. "Hit it, Rocky!"

The strains of Rachmaninoff's Variations on a Theme by Paganini came out over the boxy speakers suspended from the ceiling as Grandma's fingers flitted across the bare table, playing the unseen piano, her hands dancing across the invisible keyboard in perfect synchronization with the melody.

X sat down in the chair next to Joe, and Rocky joined her, the trio enthralled with Grandma's exhibition. Gradually, people of all ages began to file in, their boisterous outside-voices quieting to a whisper-level of respect for her performance as they entered the hall.

Just before the music ended, Rocky stood up and went to the record player, ready to shut it off before the next song came up.

X stood up and clapped when Grandma was done, the

rest of the villagers joining in as they always did when they were treated to one of Krista Rachmaninoff's performances.

"That was inspirational," X told her, then sat down next to her. "I could just about see the keys under your fingers as they flew across the table."

"One day, maybe I'll have a real piano. When the missionaries took me away from my parents as a child, telling them they couldn't care for me properly, I was sent to the Indian School. The nuns there taught me how to play a simple piece on the piano. When they saw that I could play by ear, they let me have more piano time as a reward for speaking the English. I was a fast learner. I didn't like not being able to speak Inupiaq but *did* like to make music. The other children and I used to hide under the covers and talk to each other at night, so the nuns wouldn't hear us. They were tough on us, but we were tougher. I learned how to speak English and how to play the piano, but I never forgot my Inupiaq words."

Rocky placed a chipped coffee cup filled with pennies next to X, another one just like it in front of him. He pulled out the laminated bingo cards from his jacket pocket, then hung the coat on the back of his folding chair. "How many cards do you think you can do at once?" he asked.

"I don't know. I haven't played bingo since I was a kid."

"Start her off with eight. She's a smart girl. Clever and fast, and has red hair like me, too. I like you, Alexandra."

X found herself blushing at the compliment, then looked to see if Rocky had seen it. If he had, he wasn't making a big deal out of it like she had when she had caught him blushing. *Cool! A real gentleman.*

Rocky kept his grin contained. The more he was around this woman, the more he found likable about her. She may have had an icy exterior when they first met, but it was melting fast, very fast.

He counted out eight cards, then set a dozen cards out in front of himself and his grandmother, ready for the rapid-fire game that had been the only entertainment in the village until video tapes came out. He looked up and saw the caller was ready, her thick glasses perched on the end of her snub nose, her red calico kuspuk almost as bright as her cheeks.

"Why did you bring your own cards? Don't you get new ones when you come in?"

"Nope. We've been using the same ones since I can remember. I almost don't have to look at them to see if I have the numbers. Use the pennies to mark out the spot. And don't forget to call out if you win. Or rather, Grandma wins. We're not playing. We're just marking the cards for her."

The next two hours were full of shouts of 'bingo' and 'only one more…' before the caller raised her hand. "Last game. Then we have dessert."

"What did she win?" X asked when they were done, the number of buttons the winning cards had earned almost as plentiful as the pennies.

"The buttons," Rocky said. "Or she can trade them in for trim or fabric. She and the other ladies barter for what they need, donating their extra goods as winning prizes. They'd swap with each other anyhow, but this is more fun."

The caller was now shouting, but not bingo letters and numbers. Her husband was getting chastised for something, her words in Inupiaq, not English. She looked over at X and saw she had a new audience for her bedevilment and continued her rant, now in English.

"My husband…" Marla kept on ranting and raving, peppering her English with Inupiaq words that didn't have a translation, screeching about her 'no good, worthless husband.' At least she did until Rocky walked up to her and put his hand on her shoulder.

"It's not nice to berate someone, especially in public. Isn't that what you taught me in Sunday School? At least, that's what I remember you saying."

Marla scowled, huffed in what she felt was righteous indignation, then brought up her leathery index finger and started in on Rocky. "Yes, maybe that's true in the Bible, but this is different. My husband drinks and doesn't come home when he's supposed to and…and…"

She paused, Rocky's hand on her shoulder again as he walked in front of her and squatted down to her petite height so she couldn't help but see him. He shook his head back and forth then spoke softly so only she could hear. "The Bible is for all of us. Not just men, not just righteous men, not just for women, not just for Americans, Russians, fishermen or sinners. All of us."

"Yes, but…"

Rocky put his hand up in front of her mouth and shook his head again. "Would you want to come home to a man who shouted at you and told the whole village about your faults? A man's home should be his castle. Even if it's a seal-skin covered dugout, he should feel safe. If he has a wife, she should welcome him with open arms. Remember how it was when you were first married? When he came home after a long hunt?"

Marla's mouth turned up into a sly smile as she remembered the amorous days and nights that resulted in three babies in three years. Her smile quickly disappeared when she remembered that after the third child, he hadn't spent as much time with her and she was lonely. When he did come home after working his second job and only wanted to eat then go to sleep, she was angry and lashed out. It wasn't much later that he took to drinking homemade alcohol, making it at his bachelor friend's home.

"But then he started drinking…"

"And why did he start drinking? Was it because you stopped being the loving wife you had been? After hunting and fishing with the others, he worked at the hotel, cleaning rooms to make money for electricity so you could watch your television shows. He did it out of love for you. And what did it get him?" Rocky shrugged his shoulder and grinned.

Marla scowled again. "Maybe you're a little bit right," she said, her thumb and finger close together. I give him one more chance."

Rocky shook his head. "No, you give him more than one chance. You give him one chance for every mean word you've said to him for the last three years. Or more. Love him like the man you married, not the man you forced him to become. I'd say do it for me, but I want you to do it for you. And him. And for your three daughters. They should see how a wife should treat her husband. You do this? Yes?"

Marla sighed in frustration, but she knew he was right. "Yes. I do it for him and me and my daughters." A smile suddenly bloomed on her face. "And if he's a good man again and stops drinking, maybe I let him try for that son he always wanted."

Rocky rolled his eyes, then planted a quick kiss on the top of her head. "More men in the village would be nice."

Chapter 4

"Have you ever had Eskimo ice cream?" Rocky asked, nodding to the table where Marla was now dishing out desserts, her husband at her elbow, all smiles at the prospect of a new beginning for his strained marriage.

"No, is it any different from any other ice cream?" X asked, accepting the dish of the berry-infused frozen concoction Marla's husband handed her.

"Just berries for me, please," Rocky said, nodding to the tray behind the pair.

Marla suddenly squeaked as her husband moved behind her, his one hand holding the cup of berries, the other down low to sneak an appreciative pat on her bottom.

"Thanks," Marla whispered to Rocky and handed him two spoons. "I think you give good advice."

"You're very welcome. I learned from a good teacher." He turned to X. "Don't eat it yet. Let's go sit over here."

"It looks delicious," she said as she leaned in to inspect it. "Are those blueberries?"

"Some are blueberries, but most are crowberries. I'd say

dig in, but if you've never had Eskimo ice cream, you might not like it."

"Why?" X asked, spoon poised in front of her mouth to take a big bite."

"Did you see any cows around?"

"No. What difference does that make?"

"There's no milk in it. We call it akutaq—a mix or blend of something. It's made from berries…"

X nodded, eager to eat the purplish concoction, but obeying his suggestion to wait.

"And snow…"

"How long is this going to take? I don't want it to drip on me and soil the kuspuk."

"And seal oil. This blend has some ground up white fish in it, too. It tastes great to me, but I don't think you've been around long enough to appreciate the taste of seal."

X set the spoon back in the bowl and grimaced, her stomach growling at the loss of sustenance. "Does your bowl of berries have seal or fish in it, too?"

"Nope. Do you want to trade?"

"I think you know the answer to that. Thanks for looking out for me and my chechako belly."

"Anytime."

***

X tried stifling her yawns, turning away so they weren't as obvious, but her twenty-four-hour day was catching up to her. She didn't want to be rude and ask to leave while the others were still socializing, so quietly moved away from the table and got comfortable on the bench near the door, resting her head on the coats hanging on the wall.

"Hey, sleepyhead. Let's go back to Grandma's house," Rocky said, gently moving her shoulder forward.

"Wait. What? Did I fall asleep?"

"Is that a rhetorical question?" Rocky asked, trying to keep from laughing at her.

"You and your big words, small town boy."

"I take exception to your remark, big town *girl...*"

"Oh, shoot. I insulted you again. I didn't mean to, though. It's just that small town and man don't go together," X said, rubbing her forehead, trying to make some sense out of her crazy day and how she had wound up at a church bingo game instead of catching z's in a hotel room, recuperating in solitude from the long flight from the east coast.

"You may not think it's very big, but Barrow is the biggest

village in northern Alaska. Up here in the North Slope Borough, I'm from the big city." He laughed and offered his hand to help her stand. "Come on. Grandma already left with her new boyfriend. Or old boyfriend. I'm not sure which one he is this month."

"And she'll probably never tell you. I know I wouldn't. I think that's one thing that women the world over share: they don't kiss and tell. Well, at least with folks of the opposite sex."

"I didn't bring a coat, or I'd let you wear it. Are you warm enough?"

X took two steps away from the door and felt the goose bumps rise. "How about we walk close together. I hope I don't ruin your reputation by being so bold."

"Nah, don't worry about that," Rocky said as he wrapped his arm around her shoulder, her arm reaching around his waist at the same time. "People around here have their own lives to think about. They're not concerned about me. That is, unless you were holding a knife to me or something."

X spun halfway around Rocky and poked the index finger of her free hand into his belly. "Stick 'em up! Give me all your muktuk!" she said, then laughed, gave him a quick squeeze, then kept walking toward Grandma's house, sporting a smile of contentment and peace in her new surroundings.

"I don't remember when I've had so much fun. If you had told me last week—shoot, even this afternoon—that I'd be having a blast playing bingo for buttons with a bunch of old folks and stroking a man's penis bone, I'd have asked for a head examination."

"Well, I suggest you keep the last part to yourself. Your college friends might not understand the joke, and then someone might get in trouble. Speaking of trouble," Rocky said. "We're here. Let me go inside and make sure Grandma and Joe aren't inside. Or at least, aren't playing around. I don't think she forgot you were spending the night..."

While he was inside scouting for improprieties, X noticed something sparkling in the tall grass next to the steps. She moved the blades of grass away with her boot and saw what looked like a small bowling ball of glass.

"That's a float," Rocky said. "Go ahead and bring it inside where you can see it better. Oh, and Grandma's not here. Looks like you get to sleep in her bed anyhow and I get my couch back. I'll go grab some clean sheets."

X bent down and picked up the reflective glass and held it close as she came back up the wooden steps. Stepping over the threshold, her boot snagged on the edge of the floor mat and she tumbled forward. One hand shot out to try and break her fall, the other clutched the glass globe close to her belly in a vain attempt at keeping it safe.

Splat! Crash!

"Aiyee!"

Rocky rushed out of the bedroom and saw the young woman face down on the floor, her back arched as she tried to keep from getting glass shards deeper into her belly.

She pulled her extended arm close to her body and tried to lift herself up.

"Wait! Let me help you." Rocky straddled her prone figure and grasped under her armpits, lifting her up from the floor, the blood and broken bits of glass confirming his fears. "Bring your knees up and help me get you to your feet."

Whimpering from fear rather than pain, X did as he instructed, her legs heavy and sluggish as shock began to set in. "I'm scared," she said when her feet were finally beneath her.

Then she puked. Frothy purple berries mixed with the

darkening blood on the floor, the eerie glow of the incandescent light in the corner made the room feel like a scene from a B horror movie. Her body began to shake uncontrollably, another indication of shock.

"I'll take care of you," Rocky said firmly. "It's what I do. Can you make it to the bedroom? I'll help support you, but I don't want to carry you if I don't have to. That might move more glass into your belly or what's in there, deeper."

"I can walk," she sobbed. "But I'm scared."

"You *never* have to be afraid if I'm with you, okay? Like I said, I'll take care of you."

"But my job! I'm supposed to start to work day after tomorrow…" she wailed, and her sobs continued.

"First things first," Rocky said. "I have to take off the kuspuk and your shirt and see what's happening."

"Oh, shit!" X said, holding up her bloody right hand.

Rocky grabbed the flashlight by the side of Grandma's bed and examined her hand. A large shard of glass was embedded in it. He knew that as soon as he pulled it out, the blood would be free flowing. "Lie down."

X looked behind her and saw she had made it to the front of the double bed. "Huh?"

"Don't ask. Do." He held her by her elbows and lowered her onto the bed, glad that he hadn't had a chance to strip the sheets. This was going to be messy. It looked like he'd have to buy Grandma new sheets after this ordeal.

The whimpers continued, but the protests stopped. "Hold your hand up here," Rocky said, positioning her right arm so it was bent at the elbow, fingers pointed toward the ceiling. "I don't want the blood to start flowing again. This is going to be tricky. I have to see what's going on with the other cuts before I work on your hand. And don't fall asleep! I want you to look at me."

She watched his hands as he lifted her tank top and kuspuk to examine her bloody belly. He noticed her look of terror and reworded his order, "Look at my face, not my hands and what I'm doing. Or look at my hair or ears, but don't go to sleep. Can you do that for me?"

"Yes, doctor," she said, sniffling back the tears. "You have pretty ears… I mean, you have handsome ears."

"Thanks," he mumbled, then stood up. "I'll be right back. Don't go anywhere," and gave her a mischievous smile and a wink, doing his best to cover his concern. This wasn't going to be easy or painless.

When he came back in the room, her eyes were shut, her breathing slow and regular, her right arm gently swaying back and forth as she continued to hold it upright despite being asleep. He felt her pulse. Strong and even. The mess on the living room floor was ugly, but not too widespread. She hadn't lost much blood. It would be better for them both if she stayed asleep. He took one of the towels he had brought in the room and rolled it up and set it on her upper chest, supporting the wavering arm. "You can relax your arm now," he whispered, then felt her tension ease, her hand now resting on the bundled terrycloth bolster.

While she slept, Rocky split the kuspuk up the front with the shears, then pulled out the loose pieces of glass, dropping them into the stainless steel bowl. He hated to cut into her ribbed tank top, but she'd have to make do with one of his tee shirts as an undergarment until her luggage came in. There were dozens of small pieces of glass in the fabric and lifting it away from her skin pulled many of the shards out at the same time. If only they were ferrous, he could use a strong magnet to remove them, and his task would be easier. Not today.

He could sense when she had awakened. She didn't say

a word, but her breathing rhythm changed, her flesh tensed at his touch. He looked up and smiled at her. "I have the glass out of your belly, at least as much as I can see in this light, but I still have to work on your hand. I was afraid to start on it while you were asleep. There are so many little tendons and muscles in there that if I was removing a piece of glass and you jerked, it could… Well, it could make a difference in the outcome."

"Why don't you just take me to the hospital?"

"We don't have a full-time doctor. The nurses are good, but they haven't sewed up as many cuts as I have. Besides, with all the new rules and restrictions, I don't know if they'd even work on you. They'd probably call in an air evac and ship you to Fairbanks or Anchorage. Since you're not Native and wouldn't be getting free medical, you'd have to have some mighty good health insurance to cover the cost of a charter flight."

Rocky watched as X's eyes widened while he explained his reasoning. He was telling the truth, but he'd still rather work on her than let the young new intern see her. His need to protect her was surging the more time he spent with her. He felt as if he was only a millimeter away from claiming her as his own. Every time he touched her skin, it felt as if his soul was growing a new layer, that he had been missing this last covering and she was it, adding to his spirit even in her weakened, unconscious state. What would it be like if she felt the same way, if they touched and held each other as lovers…

"Rocky, why are your ears red?"

"Huh?"

"You told me to look at your ears. All of the sudden, they're crimson. Guys don't get hot flashes, do they?"

"Sometimes. Sorta. They're more like tsunamis…" Rocky sat up and arched his back. "I did the best I could for now. The smaller pieces will work themselves out over time. Now that you're awake, I want to soak some gauze in peroxide and swipe it across your belly. One reason, of course, is for use as a disinfectant. The other is that small glass bits will catch on the gauze and, hopefully, get pulled out. Now, this is going to tickle or hurt, depending on how you perceive it. Either way, it'll feel cold."

"Why didn't you… Oh, yeah. Thanks for waiting until I woke up to do this part. I don't know what I would have done if I awoke with a whole new set of sensations."

"The first thing you would have done is probably grabbed for my hand, trying to get it away, using your injured and dominant right hand. That probably would have sent you right over the edge in pain and frustration and maybe even caused more damage, driving the glass in deeper or wider. Are you ready for this?" he asked, the peroxide-saturated gauze pad dripping over the bowl.

"No, but I'd better be. I think I'll watch your eyes this time. You sure have long, straight eyelashes… Ouch!"

"Should I stop?"

"No, let's get it over with. I know the hand is next. Man, I wish I had a drink! And I'm not a drinker, either."

X's abdominal muscles clenched—and so did her jaws—as Rocky finished his disinfectant swabbing. She knew he saw the old and faded scars on her lower belly, but he never said a word. He had to be curious, though. Depending on how severe her new wounds were, she wouldn't even have a four-inch patch of unscarred belly. Not that she'd ever want to wear a bikini again. Even crop tops were probably out of the question now. Of course, if she ever moved to a cold climate, that wouldn't be a problem. Barrow was a nice place and Rocky was a nice man…

And she was out.

"Hey, wake up. I know you're tired, but I can't work on your hand while you're asleep. I do know where Grandma's stash of berry and vanilla rheumatism medicine is, though. Would you care to try a little of that before I get started? It might ease the pain a bit."

"Yes, I think a little preventative medicine might help. It's only throbbing now, but I know once you get into it, the pain will start all over again."

Rocky glanced at her belly. "Looks like you're familiar with pain," and nodded, a slight smile of appreciation showing on his tired face. "I'll be right back. She keeps it under the sink with the cleansers."

As soon as he was out of the room, X sat up and looked at her bared belly. Rocky had laid a brown-knit shawl across her bared bosom. He had either taken the trouble to unhook her foam-enhanced pushup bra or cut it off. Either way, he now knew she was nearly flat chested, her curvy shape the result of a thirty-dollar foundation garment. Beyond the shawl, she saw his handiwork—a three-inch wound below and to the right of her bellybutton—stitched with at least twenty stitches. Three other shorter wounds were also stitched closed, the black knotted threads appearing like small ants in short marching lines. She relaxed her neck, letting her head plop down on the feather pillow, sinking into its softness and into despair at the same time. How long had she been unconscious? The brown paper over the windows masked out the twenty-four hours of daylight and there wasn't a clock visible in her line of sight.

And poor Rocky. The fatigue sapped the sassiness from his face, aging him at least ten years with lines of worry. Still, if that's how he was going to age, he'd be a great-looking older man. *Why are you fantasizing over him? Yes, he's a great guy, but…*

"Are you okay? You look mad," he said, sitting back down on the three-legged stool he'd been using as his surgeon's seat for the last four hours.

"My mad face looks just like my frustrated face, probably because I get mad when I'm frustrated and am frustrated that I get mad." She laughed despite herself. *You certainly can't tell him you're getting the hots for him and frustrated that you know it'd never work out!*

"It's too bad you had to cut the kuspuk. I liked it."

"Kuspuks come and go," he said, then finished his

thought in his head, *'But you're a once in a lifetime woman.'* He cleared his throat and added out loud, "And I have a few more hanging on the wall, ready to personalize for you."

"Patched up, just like me?"

"You have a lot of life left in you, too." He showed her the coffee cup, half-full of homemade liquor. "I think I'll need to lift your head, so you can drink. I'm sure your tummy muscles are tender." He set the cup on the nightstand and stood up, leaning over to assist her. "Ready?"

She tipped her head forward and he slid his hand beneath her left shoulder, bringing her forward enough that she could sip the berry juice and vanilla extract concoction.

"Oh, my, that's good! More..." She leaned forward, urging him to tilt the cup by sticking out her chin.

"It's stronger than you think. And if you're not a drinker like you say, it's gonna kick your butt."

She stuck her tongue into the cup, trying to get the last drop out of it before he pulled it away. "I got drunk once and that was enough. Never again. I'll drink one glass of wine or champagne in a toast, but that's it. I don't even like the taste of beer, so I pass at barbecues and parties." She scowled at the loss of sweet drink and licked her lips, wanting more.

"How about you? Do you drink?"

"I gave in to peer pressure and tried it once, and that was one time too many. I'm pretty sure there's a genetic weakness for it. I've seen it around here enough. I don't smoke, either. Why even try that? I can't see anything wrong with drinking Grandma's home brew as a medicine, though— at least in this case—because I need you to relax. If you're not tense, my work is a lot easier. Can you imagine where we'd be if you fell and got hurt and we were both drunk? You'd probably still be in the living room, lying in a pool of blood. You'd survive, most likely, but you'd have a rougher recovery. Plus, I'd feel horrible for not being able to take care of you."

"Can you add a little water to the cup? Suddenly, I'm real thirsty."

Rocky poured water from the nightstand ewer into the cup, swirled it around to capture the last drops of liquor, then bent forward and lifted her shoulders again, this time allowing himself to sniff her hair, the aroma reviving his resolve to get this finished before Grandma showed up. He still had to clean up the mess in the living room, too. His shoulders sagged as he lay her back down on the pillow. It was becoming the longest day in more than one way.

"Are you sure you shouldn't make a pot of coffee before you start?" X asked, patting his knee with her uninjured left hand.

He held up the can of cola that was beside the ewer. "Caffeine in a can, plus a sugar kick. I have more in the pantry if needed. How are you feeling now?"

X giggled and poked her uninjured index finger into her cheek. "Soft and silly. Is that good?"

He took her hand from her face, patted it gently, and tucked it under her hip. "That works for both of us. Keep your hand down so you don't reach out and slap me without thinking." He scowled and amended his phrase. "Or punch me intentionally. This isn't going to be fun for either of us."

She giggled again. "Okay. But promise me we'll have fun again soon." She winked at him and grinned. "And this time I want more fun than just playing bingo for buttons!"

Puzzled but intrigued at the possibility that she was flirting, he pasted on his conciliatory smile and said, "I promise," his doubting second-nature shouting, *'It's the alcohol making her horny. She'll forget about you in the morning.'*

Rocky picked up the stool and went to the other side of the bed. His patient was very relaxed, singing and humming random tunes as he examined the angle of how the glass shard had entered her hand. If he could pull it out the same way, there'd be less damage.

"I'm going to pull out the big piece," he said, interrupting her song of Happy Birthday to Me. "It's going to hurt. I have something that might help, though. Bite on this. It's what my patients use. It helps to keep them focused and not lashing out."

"What is it?" she asked, trying to figure out what the long brown object he held was.

"I call it my anesthetist, but it's just a length of walrus hide, too tough to bite through."

"Are those teeth marks from other people?" she asked, her stomach rumbling at the thought of chewing on anything that had been in other people's mouths, especially the back end of a two-ton sea mammal.

He leaned close to her face to look at it from her point of view, wanting to be near a part of her that was uninjured. "Yup." He sat back, then offered it to her again. "Here, hold onto it, just in case. Once I get into doing this, I won't be able to let go and give it to you."

"Good grief!" X exclaimed as she took the eight-inch long by inch-and-a-half wide strip of tough leather. "This thing's heavier than it looks."

"It's because it's denser. It was thicker twenty-two years ago when my grandmother gave it to my mother to bite down on when she was delivering me."

"Ew! What an heirloom. I think I'll only need to hold onto it."

"Whatever works," Rocky said, then bent over her hand, restrained at her wrist with a belt strapped to his knee. He took out a fresh pair of gloves and slipped them on, saying a quick silent prayer as he always did when gloving up.

Giving her his best smile of confidence, he said, "I'll make this as quick as I can."

"I'd prefer as painless as you can," she said. "I really don't want to use your anesthetist," and twirled it between her fingers.

"I'll do both. Stick it under your hip for now so you don't use it to whack me with. Ready?"

X turned her head, slipped the hide and her hand under her left butt cheek, and took a deep breath. "Go for it, Doc."

Rocky bit his bottom lip as he quickly tugged on the glass shard. It wouldn't budge.

He felt her back arch at the pain, but she didn't cry out or try to jerk away from him.

"Hold on. I have to rinse off the dried blood. Your body's already trying to heal around it." Rather than squirt his limited supply of peroxide on it and cause her even more pain, Rocky grabbed the bottle of saline eye wash from the table, his go-to sterile solution.

"Again," he said, and pulled. It didn't come free.

"Shit! I have to try one more time."

He heard her sniff at the pain, her hiccups of sobs being swallowed by her determination not to cry out.

"Got it!"

"Can I have another drink now?" X asked, raising the back of her left hand—still clutching The Anesthetist—to wipe under her nose.

"No. You'd just throw it up. I don't want that and neither do you." Rocky saw her disappointment but knew he had to be tough. It was hard for her and even worse for him. She may have liked him a few minutes ago—even flirted with him, entertaining a little one-on-one happy time together—but she would probably be on the next plane before her first twenty-four hours in Barrow was over.

"I know that was uncomfortable, but now I have to clean it. If I don't, you might get an infection. I have antibiotics—and believe me when I say I have more experience in hand surgeries than a lot of doctors—but if I don't get all the tiny bits of glass and debris out, you'll have to have another surgery, at best."

"And at worst, I'll lose my hand?" she asked, sniffling and wiping her nose again.

"You're pretty smart, even when you're a little drunk."

"Certified genius. Flat-chested, red-haired, stuck-up genius."

"Shut up and bite The Anesthetist. Nobody but you cares about labels, and I'm not too sure you really do, either." He quickly poured the peroxide over the wound, grasping her wrist as he did so, making sure she didn't pull free from the leather belting.

"Um!" she shrieked, the walrus leather extending from either side of her mouth like a starched mustache. Her feet twisted and turned, her knees pulling up halfway until he elbowed the right one down, telling her sharply, "No!"

Just as he was ready to give in to his sympathies and let up on the probing for more debris, he found another shard. He grabbed it with the forceps and set it down, squirting the area with saline one more time to flush away the new blood that had been blocked by the glass. Satisfied that the cleansing was done, he blotted the excess away and began the arduous task of stitching. It would be easier to take fewer stitches, but he had enough suture, and this was a woman. A lady. She didn't need or want a Frankenstein scar on her dainty hand, even on the inside of it. He wasn't a plastic surgeon, but he'd give it his best shot.

Half an hour later, Rocky took off his gloves and dropped them in the trash by his side.

"Do you hate me?" he asked when he removed the leather strap from her mouth.

"Are you done hurting me?" she replied, her eyes still red from crying.

He looked to the box of tissues on the nightstand, pulled a couple out, and held them up. "Except for this," he said and wiped her nose. "It looks a little red under there. Better?"

"The nose, yes. And I know you had to do it. Shoot! When did you start doing this? You act as if it's all in a day's work for you."

"Since I was about eight, I think. My first patient was a dog, though. After that, the men took me out fishing as the medic. I was too small to haul anything in, but I was good at cutting bait. Pretty soon, they figured out that it was better to leave me on shore so if someone got hurt on a different boat, I'd be available. Kinda hard to get the word out sometimes. Besides, most of the injuries happened on land, while they were hauling in the catch or processing it. Worked for me because I don't care to be on the water."

"So, is that what you want to do? Become a doctor?"

"Some folks are called to be healers, no matter where they live. My options are pretty limited here. I might be able to get a scholarship to cover the cost of college, but," he shrugged a shoulder, uncomfortable with the topic, then had a thought. "Wait here," he said and winked. "I'll be right back with something for you."

X looked at her right hand, now tethered to the metal headboard with a series of ropes and knots. "As if I could go anywhere."

Rocky walked back in with the bottle of liquor and a straw. He filled her coffee cup half full and set the straw into it, holding it up to her so she could drink from her reclined position. When he was sure she had finished swallowing it, he set it down, then knelt beside her. "Don't worry," he whispered, "I won't tell anyone I had my way with you in bed."

X snorted a chuckle that quickly became a full laugh. "Oh, I so needed that," she said when she calmed down enough to talk.

"Needed what? Me to have my way with you in bed or my doctoring skills? It'd better be one or the other, because if you're making a joke out of me as a lover…"

Rocky stood up suddenly, his words evaporating into the chill of his insecurities. "I gotta go clean up the mess before Grandma comes back. You need to rest."

"Rocky," X said, her voice calm and compassionate, "I'd love to have you in my bed. I appreciate your skills as a doctor and I have no doubt that you're just as wonderful and caring in making love. When you're done cleaning up that horrid mess I made, would you come lie down with me?"

He nodded. For the first time in years, he wanted to cry. Whether it was from shame at being seen as a lesser man by a woman he was quickly falling for or from fatigue and exasperation he didn't know. But he did know he had to tell someone what he was up to or burst. Was she the one, though?

Chapter 5

"I thought you were going to lie down with me," X said when Rocky came in to take a blanket out of the closet.

He shrugged as he held the crocheted afghan close, his arms crossed in front of his chest, unintentionally miming protecting his heart. He became aware of his body language and set it lower, protecting his manhood instead. He shifted it again to his hip. *Danged psychology books! Now what in the heck does this mean—that I'm beside myself in confusion?*

"You look uncomfortable," X said. "I know you're tired. I've waited up this long for you; please, don't make me beg you to come lie down with me. I really am scared, and you said you'd take care of me."

"You remember that?" he said, then came to her left side, setting the afghan down to use as his pillow.

"I think I remember everything you've ever said to me, including putting me in my place for jumping to conclusions when you were rolling those asthma cigarettes."

"As I recall, I said judging others on outward appearances," and turned to face her.

She shifted to face him, then grunted, the wounds in her belly screaming for attention now that her hand wasn't throbbing as much. "I forgot about the cuts in my belly," she said. "How many were there?"

"Only four that required sutures. The others were just shallow surface cuts."

"How long will I hurt?"

"As long as you're thinking about them plus a day. The extra day is because your mind will remember the pain and will want the attention. The brain is funny that way."

Rocky had picked up her left arm as he spoke, gently touching her skin, following her nerve paths from her elbow to her wrist, gently massaging the base of her hand, then rubbing her fingers up to her fingertips, bringing the blood flow back to her chilly hand.

"I'll let you do that all night, Rocky," she said dreamily.

"Can't do that," he said, not even trying to hide his orneriness.

"Why not?"

"Because it's morning," he said, then brought her hand to his face and breathed in, stopping short of kissing it.

She had fallen asleep.

And there was no way he'd share a first kiss—even one on the hand—with an unconscious woman.

***

"What happened here? And where is my new rug?" Grandma called out.

"Oh, shoot," Rocky said, and rolled out of bed and bounded to the door. "Stay put," he called behind him, just in case X had been awakened, too.

"Couldn't go anywhere if I tried," she mumbled, then let her head loll to the other side, wishing she was asleep again and pain-free.

"There was an accident, Grandma. I took the rug out to the dumpster. And it wasn't a new rug. You got that when I was in the first grade. I'll buy you another one."

"What kind of accident?" She sniffed the air. "It smells like a hospital in here. Did you kill someone?"

"What? No!" Rocky shook his head, trying to clear his thoughts. He looked at the clock on the wall. It was eight o'clock. He'd only been asleep two hours.

"Grandma, I'll have to replace that old glass float you kept in the yard, too. I told Alexandra she should bring it in the house if she wanted a closer look and she tripped. She cut her hand and her belly pretty bad."

"You fixed her up, though, right?"

Rocky nodded, then looked around. Something wasn't right. "Grandma, where's your cane?"

"Oh, I let Joe borrow it. He said he'd use it as a pattern to build me another one."

"Grandma, you and I both know that if he was going to carve you another cane, all he had to do was measure the length of that one."

Grandma giggled behind her hand like a teenager. "Yup. He knows and I know and you know… It just gives me an excuse to go visit him again. I like him."

"Sometimes I think you like Joe too much and other times…" He shook his head, frustrated. "You're either fighting or loving on each other. You two need to either get married or call it quits."

"I can't marry him!" she said, her arm raised, ready to slam her walking stick into the floor. When she remembered she no longer had it, she planted her knuckles into her hips instead.

"Why can't you marry Joe, Grandma?" Rocky asked, exasperated because he knew she had taunted him into asking her.

"Because we're already married! He was my first and only husband!" she said, then laughed as she headed toward the kitchen.

She stopped in the archway and turned around. "Where's your new girlfriend? I like her. She reminds me of me."

"That's what you keep saying. And she's not my girlfriend. She's the lady with lost luggage and a missing hotel reservation who's here to help with the archaeological dig."

"That's what *you* keep saying," she mocked, and continued into the kitchen. He heard a cabinet door shut, then the rest of them slam one after the other. "Who took my rheumatism medicine?"

"I did, and you don't need it. She does. Why don't you go back and see Joe?"

She looked into the living room, one hand holding the wall for support. "Good idea. He should be rested up by now. He's not as young as he used to be, but I am! See you tomorrow. Maybe. Have fun with your 'not my girlfriend!'"

X waited until she heard the door shut behind Grandma

before calling out. "Come on back to bed. I promise I won't bite. Or growl. I might snore, though."

"So, you heard everything we said?" he asked when he walked in.

"Kind of hard not to." She patted the bed next to her, her slight smile letting him know she wouldn't bring up the topic of girlfriend/not my girlfriend.

He lay back down, but rest wouldn't come for either of them. The awkward silence grew until X asked, "What you did with my hand, would it work on my belly?"

"Probably, why?"

"Duh! Because I want to feel good. I hurt all over and right now, if you could make my sliced and diced gut feel better, maybe I'd forget about my hand. I mean," she toned down her frustration and started again. "I guess you could do it on my feet, but I'm ticklish and I'd hate to think either one of us had a foot fetish. I can't roll over, so you can't give me a back massage. And above my belly... Well, I don't know you that well..."

Rocky reached up and touched the side of her neck, watching as the goosebumps raced down her body, disappearing under the shawl until they reappeared on her bared belly. "You mean here?"

"No, that's not where I meant, but…"

He continued with his light touch, adding a gentle pressure when he felt her pulse quicken.

"That'll do," she gasped. "I owe you one. Or two."

He squirmed, trying to get comfortable now that he had become aroused. He didn't want to reach down and rearrange his bits and pieces and let her know what feeling her skin did to him.

"Or three or however much you want," she sighed, her bottom rocking back and forth in pleasure.

"You need rest," he whispered in her ear, letting her hair tickle his nose, welcoming the distraction from what she was doing to the rest of him without even trying.

"So do you," she replied in the same lusty whisper. "I don't know if it's a good thing that I'm hurting or not, but your touch is driving me nuts. If I wasn't all cut up and tied down, you wouldn't have a chance…"

"That's just the pain and alcohol talking. I won't hold it against you later."

X's left hand reached around and pulled him close to her, the front of his corduroy jeans now snuggled up to the side of her hip. "Then hold it against me now. Just because I'm not ready doesn't mean I'm not wanting." She tugged him close, pulsing her one-armed hug three times. "And I can tell you're wanting, too."

Rocky let his hand drift down to her waist, away from the erogenous zones on her neck to a possible tickle zone below her ribs. She flinched, but then relaxed into him, her squirms continuing. "Another day, another time, perhaps," he whispered.

"Another day, another time, for sure," she whispered back, then fell asleep, at peace for the first time that she could remember.

***

The blare of the alert siren awakened both of them, X screeching in pain as soon as consciousness hit.

"I have to go," Rocky said, as he jumped out of the bed, looking around, trying to orient himself with where he was.

He ran his fingers through his hair, still confused, then noticed X, her wounded hand still tied to the bedframe. "It's an emergency," he explained as he untied the knots. "I'll be

87

back as soon as I can. Don't go anywhere. I mean, don't leave the house."

He ran to the door and slipped on his boots. "I promise, I'll be back as soon as I can."

"But...but..." X called out after the shut door, "I don't know where the bathroom is."

As soon as she tried to sit up, she regretted it. X automatically reached for the tender belly with her wounded right hand and yowled. Frustration fueled her pain until she gave in to it and chanted, "Shit! Shit! Shit! No spilled food, but shit! Shit! Shit! Where's a knight is shining armor when you need help getting to the bathroom. Shit! Shit! Shit!"

"Um, do you need some help?"

X looked up and saw a familiar face. "Q?"

"Yup, that's me. I came by to see Grandma. Are you all right?"

She waved her bandaged hand, pink-tinged with blood, at him. "Do I look all right to you?" The scarf that had been draped across her chest for modesty started to slip. She grasped for it, clutching it close to her with her left hand.

"No, you look horrible. Sorry, but you do. I heard the siren, so I know Rocky's gone, but where's Grandma?"

"I'll tell you if you let me know where the bathroom is around this place. I haven't peed since yesterday afternoon and my eyes are floating."

Q started to laugh at the old joke told by a young white woman sitting in his grandmother's bed with nothing on but a qiviut shawl. "I'm sorry, but all we have here is the outhouse out back and the honey bucket. It's over there in the corner," he said, pointing to the five-gallon bucket with a lid on it and a roll of toilet paper on the dresser next to it. "Do you need a hand?" he asked, taking a step inside the bedroom, his eyes lighting up, hoping the shawl would slip and he'd get a peek at more bared skin.

She shook her head, and said, "No, thanks. I'll manage. Grandma is at Joe's house. I'd knock before entering, though. I think they're rekindling their old flame...again."

"It's safer to walk in on them if they're rekindling rather than re-feuding. Grandma tends to throw things when she gets mad. That's why we don't let her keep breakables inside."

"Like glass globes?" X asked, raising her hand.

"Did you break Grandma's Japanese float? She's gonna be sooo mad..."

"She didn't seem to mind this morning. Now, if you don't mind, I'd like a little time to myself…"

"Oh, yeah—the honey bucket. Sorry we don't have the fancy accommodations the hotel does. Did you ever get your hotel reservations sorted out?"

"Q! Leave! Now! Before I wet Grandma's bed!" X shouted, shooing him away with her good hand.

"Okay. Tell Grandma I have a question about potlatch," he called out as he shut the door.

"Potluck? I didn't know Natives had potlucks?"

After relieving herself in the clean but years' old container, Alexandra Oppenheimer realized how stranded she was. Not only was she not wearing any clothes other than her socks and bikini briefs, she didn't have any to put on! The kuspuk she had been loaned and the clothes she had been wearing since she left Logan International Airport in Boston on Friday morning—some 48 hours ago—were nowhere to be seen. Now it was Sunday. Rocky had said there was no way she'd get her lost luggage until Monday.

Her frustration was interrupted by an 'aha' moment. He had also said the brightly-colored kuspuks hanging on the hooks in the kitchen were his to reclaim. Well, if he wasn't here to help her, she'd have to help herself. Even ripped and worn clothes were better than no clothes at all.

X pawed through the cotton garments until she found one that felt soft and didn't have any obvious major tears. A few L-shaped tears were acceptable and wouldn't affect her modesty. Leaving it on the hook, she scooted underneath it, using her left hand to guide her bandaged right hand into the sleeve. After that, dressing was a breeze. She still had her panties on, confirmation that Rocky really was a gentleman and hadn't taken liberties. Her bra was another matter. By the scratches on her upper abdomen, it appeared her foam-filled bra had borne the brunt of some of the glass breakages. Undoubtedly, it was unwearable now that it was peppered with shards.

Her tummy grumbled, reminding her it had been a long time since a substantial meal. Her first thought was to walk to the convenience store and try out some canned meat. Unfortunately, with her hand all bungled up, she wouldn't be able to open it. Besides, if Q had just dropped in, the store might not be open on Sundays. Plus, she had been told to stay put by Rocky.

The thought of Rocky gave her a warm flush all over that

settled in her loins. What was it about this man? He was a stranger, had some crazy relatives, and lived in one of the most remote places on earth, even if he did claim he was from 'the big city.' He didn't have any of the attributes of the guys she'd always been attracted to in the past. She chuckled. That was probably a good thing. Pretty boys, athletic types, high IQ nerds: they were all self-absorbed. Rocky? He'd drop everything to help someone, even someone who'd been marginally rude to him. And he'd run to help a body in distress, even if there was a good possibility he'd get laid if he just stayed where he was. In bed with a warm, very willing but slightly out of it woman.

And there it was. He was generous. Okay. That's one point. But he wouldn't take liberties with an incapacitated woman. Yes, she was awake when she felt his breath on her hand. She waited for the kiss that never came, then fell asleep. Was he gay? Not hardly. She giggled at the word, the mental image of him reluctant to press up against her body, even when she pulled him close.

He was respectful. Yup! That was it. Generous, respectful, and with a touch that drove her wild.

But he was reluctant. Hesitant. Unwilling? Why?

And then she fell for him hard all over again for the first time. He knew she wanted him out of lust. Sure, they could have had a good time, even before she was injured. They had fun at the bingo game, laughing, joking. It would have been easy to carry it over in the deserted house when they got back, but then what?

Even if they both would have enjoyed a fling, that's not what he wanted. He wanted something lasting.

Red Raven. His friends Oscar and Lisa had asked if she was his Red Raven. He was holding out for 'the one.' Maybe she was attracted to him because he was so chaste in his search.

Or he could be just playing hard to get.

Nah.

He was the kind of man she wanted to spend the rest of her life with, even if it meant using a bucket as a toilet.

Chapter 6

"Are you here?" Rocky called from the front door.

X answered from the bedroom, "Come see for yourself." She rearranged her hand-me-down blue kuspuk for the umpteenth time, her bare feet crossed at the ankles seductively. Or at least at what she hoped looked appealing.

"Whoa! You look much better than last night or even an hour ago. Did you get anything to eat?"

X pointed to the empty bag of chips and the partial bottle of water beside it. "It's the only food I recognized. By the way, Q came by and said something about the potluck."

"You mean potlatch?"

"Yeah, that's the word he used, but I thought he meant potluck. Are they the same thing?"

"A potlatch is like a potluck on steroids. Usually it's in celebration of an event like a wedding or a funeral. Lots of good food, but gifts are often exchanged, too. We usually have at least one in the winter, but I think Grandma wants to have one 'just because.' Sometimes I don't know about that woman."

"Alzheimer's?"

"No. Ornery-heimer's. Or maybe she's related to the Oppenheimers." Rocky said, then smiled and winked, letting her know he remembered her last name. "Are you missing a grandmother? Or do you want one maybe? Not too many years on this one and she's only been used—gently—by one grandchild: me."

"I'd love to have your grandmother as mine. My mother and her mother stopped talking years ago. I've been forbidden to contact her. It's too bad, too. I really loved my Grandma Lou."

"How old are you?" Rocky asked, then sat down on the stool beside her, trying to ignore her obviously staged entreaty for him to join her in bed, and instead took her bandaged hand and examined it for excess seepage.

"I'm twenty-one. Why?"

"You're legal in every state in the country and old enough to make your own decisions. If you want to talk to your grandmother, talk to her. Simple as that."

"But you don't know my mother. She'd make my life miserable."

"Why? It's your life. Only you can give someone

permission to make you unhappy. She had her chance to be twenty-one; now it's your turn."

"I never thought of it that way. You're right, though. She's been dictating to me what to wear, study, even what hand lotion to use, since I can remember. She's a master at guilting people into doing what she wants. She gets all weepy if I want to do something other than what 'proper people' do."

"She'd probably cry until she ran out of tears if she saw you now, lying in a bed in a one-bedroom house in an Alaskan village, wearing a hand-me-down kuspuk with a Native man at your side, tending to your every need."

"*Every* need?" X asked and rubbed her elbow against his thigh, intentionally changing the mood from silly to, hopefully, romantic.

"I wasn't gone that long," he said, putting her elbow back at her side, setting her hand upright, "which means you're still under the influence of Grandma's berry happy juice. I would never take liberties with a woman who wasn't fully aware of what she's doing. Besides, you need to rest and so do I."

X sighed, frustrated on more than one level. "Well, part of me is mad at you for not wanting me, and another part is glad you're looking out for me, even if it isn't your job."

Rocky leaned forward, just inches from her face, and whispered, "Looking out for each other is everyone's job. Or should be. Part of that means giving up what we want in order to do what's right. Believe me, I'm doing what's right, not what I want."

X brought her left hand up and giggled into it. "That makes me feel better. I promise not to assault you if you lie down with me." She frowned. "At least, I'll try not to. You have my permission to stop me from doing anything that makes you uncomfortable. Or unhappy."

In answer, Rocky picked up the disheveled afghan from the chair, refolded it into a pillow, then lay down on his side facing her, and stifled a yawn.

"What was that siren about?"

"Little Ben again. He's only fourteen and taller than me. He was playing mumblety peg and stabbed his hand. This time, his father took the knife away from him. I told him it was a good thing he did because otherwise, I would have. I was running out of sutures!"

"Rocky," X said softly as she stared at the ceiling. She reached down and picked up his hand, then rubbed his palm with her thumb. She sighed at the sensation. It felt as if her spirit was being sated, her soul nourished by unseen energies flowing through his soft yet tough skin to hers. She wanted to ask him if he really was attracted to her, then remembered his admonishment about her having imbibed alcohol. She swallowed her original question and changed from seeking romance to being silly. "You never did tell me why you're called Rocky. You don't look like a boxer to me," she said and giggled nervously.

"It's Sergei."

She turned her head towards him. "How's Rocky a nickname for Sergei?"

"My name's Sergei Rachmaninoff. And no, I don't play the piano."

"Huh?"

"It's a classical music joke. He was a composer— concertos, symphonies, long hair music. We're probably related somehow or other—not that I can prove it. Nor that I'd want to. Like my grandmother said, we're part Russian. The men who came over and forced themselves on our culture— and women—weren't invited."

"And neither was I…" she said, and dropped his hand.

He picked it up again. "I think someone from the borough

did ask for specialists to help with the excavation, but sometimes kismet is involved, too."

"I know Kismet was a play, but what is it exactly?"

"Let's just say the two of us—lying here together, maybe even wanting each other—is kismet. A happy accident that no one could have predicted."

"Illogical but potentially wonderful."

"Certified genius," he said, squeezing her hand and bringing it close to his chest. "But I really need to get some sleep."

His head lolled back, the slow thump-thump, thump-thump of his heart letting her know he had fallen asleep. She knew what kismet was, but now she knew he felt the same way about her.

Thump-thump, thump-thump. She felt her heart pace his and concentrated on the warmth and comfort of his closeness. They were in synch. Connected. She sighed one last time and fell into a contented, pain-free slumber.

***

"You two going to sleep all day?" Grandma hollered from

the bedroom doorway.

"Not if you keep coming in and shouting," Rocky mumbled and pulled part of the afghan over his head.

"Why are you in bed with 'not your girlfriend' with your clothes on? Something wrong with you?"

"We were up all night, mending cut bodies or being mended. We're just trying to catch up."

Grandma snickered.

"On sleep, Grandma. If there's something you need in here, go ahead and get it, but leave us alone."

"Sassy boy!" She poked him under the chin with her new walking stick, showing him the narwhal carved into the handle.

Rocky pulled the cover off his head. "I'll look at it closer later but only if you leave me alone."

"I'll tell you the good news, then you can go back to *sleep*," she said and giggled at her last word.

He pulled the afghan off his head. "Go ahead. I know you won't leave me alone until you do."

She poked him in the hip with her cane. "Why you sleep with a pretty woman with your pants on? Are you sure you're my grandson?"

"You'd know better than I would," he said. "Now, what's so important?"

"I'm moving in with Joe. You and 'not your girlfriend' can have the house. I have everything I need already." She wiggled her fanny and grinned. "Joe keeps everything he needs with him all the time, too," then hummed, "Uh huh!"

"Congratulations, Grandma," Rocky said, then mumbled, "again," so only X could hear him.

Clomp! Clomp! Clomp! Grandma made her way to her rocking chair noisily, grabbed her bag of yarn and crochet project, and was out the door without another word.

"What was that all about?" X asked.

"She moves in with him every few months. It might last an hour or a month, depending on whether alcohol is involved. Joe's nephew moved to Fairbanks, so his booze supplier isn't around anymore. I hid the last of Grandma's rheumatism medicine, so they might make it a month or more this time. They manage to keep themselves happy longer when liquor isn't involved."

Rocky sat up and ran his hand through his hair and yawned. "I don't think I'll be able to go back to sleep knowing that she'll be back at least three more times for 'one more thing I forgot.'"

Clomp! Clomp! Clomp!

And there she was again.

"I forgot my wooden spoon. Sometimes Joe's a naughty boy and needs to get spanked."

Rocky rolled his eyes and said softly, "Only two more to go..."

"I heard that!" Grandma called, then stomped out the door.

"How old is she? And how long has she needed a cane?"

"Grandma's only about fifty, or so I've estimated. She was only about sixteen when she had my mother and my mother was about the same age when she had me. And as far as the cane, she doesn't need it. I think it's a prop so she can justify the need for her medicine. I've seen her dance around the room first thing in the morning when even I'm stiff."

X giggled into her bandaged hand, then cleared her throat.

Rocky copied her throat-clearing and amended his statement with a pink tinge of embarrassment. "First thing in the morning when even I'm achy."

"Might have something to do with sleeping on the couch." X rolled over on her side and watched Rocky as he stretched, ready to start the day at two in the afternoon. "So, if you're going to be at this place by yourself, would you mind having a roommate?"

The dimple on the right side of Rocky's face deepened, then disappeared as he realized he might be leaving before she did. "We'll see. You might want to get in touch with the hotel before making a final decision, though. Life can get crazy around this house."

"I don't mind. Crazy can be good." She held up her bound hand. "And I promise to be more careful with breakable objects and loose rugs."

***

"Ah, I think I found the problem," the hotel clerk said. He winked at Rocky, noticing the auburn-haired college girl in the faded blue kuspuk standing elbow-to-elbow, almost holding onto him. Looks like his old classmate finally found his red raven.

"It appears that Dr. Jackson had the single room for you cancelled, but at the same time, upgraded his reservation to a king-sized bed and added a second guest. And yes, the guest's name was Alexandra Oppenheimer."

X grunted and shook her head, the feral sound coming from her throat causing both Rocky and the clerk to stifle their laughs.

"I take it that he did that without your knowledge or permission…"

X looked at the clerk and snarled, "What was your first hint?" then grimaced in embarrassment at her snippiness. She shook her head. "I can't believe the nerve of that man! He'll probably claim cost-cutting as the reason."

"Sounds to me more like bull moose rutting," the clerk said.

Rocky shook his head at his friend in silent admonishment.

"Oops! I'm sorry, Ms. Oppenheimer. That was inappropriate."

A full laugh escaped from her this time. "It may be inappropriate, but it's very accurate. Well, sir, I thank you for your help in solving the mystery. Tell me, was my room prepaid by the university?"

He looked through the index cards and pulled one of them out. "Only the first two days. Looks like the funds were transferred over to the upgrade on his room."

Rocky put his hand on her shoulder. "Either they didn't think you'd last too long on the project or that you'd wind up in his room within that time."

"I sure wish someone would do something about sexual harassment. It took years for women to get the vote, and we're still trying to get equal pay for equal work, but the idea that we're just bubble-headed playthings—eager to please the first man who makes a pass at us, that we're willing to put out to get ahead—simply just won't go away. It's 1994 and enough is enough!"

"You're just living in the wrong culture," the clerk said. "Most Native Americans have had a matriarchal society since, well, forever."

"Good," X said. "Then there's hope for the human race. I'm beginning to feel like I was born near the wrong ocean. It should have been the Arctic, not the Atlantic."

"Never too late to move," the clerk said and winked.

X blushed, then grinned. She took Rocky's elbow,

"Come on. Let's take a walk and maybe I can get rid of some of this anger. Dr. Jackass, ergh!"

After walking for a few minutes, X's rage had subsided, her face upturned into the afternoon breeze in a smile. The ocean was still two blocks away, but she could feel the salty moistness on her cheeks, washing away her frustration. Curiosity piqued, she pointed to the three houses in a row with what looked like pelts hanging over the wooden fences. "Are those what I think they are?" she asked.

"If you think they're seals, yes. You didn't think folks around here got all their food from Q's mini market or the big store, did you?"

"No, I guess not. It looks like a bountiful harvest of animals instead of corn or grapes."

"We don't have grapes, but next month the berries will be ripe. Families will pack up and go out to the fish camps to bring in fish and gather fruit. There's lots of food around here if you know when and where to get it."

"And how to preserve it, I'm sure. I never thought about how you got the seal oil for the Eskimo ice cream. Pretty sure you use it for lots of other stuff, too."

"Cooking, heating, lighting... Before electricity, that's

106

what we used for heat and light. It's light all day long at this time of year, but in the winter, it's dark—or at least twilight—both day and night for two solid months. Even when the sun does come back up in late January," Rocky put one arm around her and pointed to the south with the other, "it hangs low on the horizon, just a distant red ball, sneaking a peak at the sky from just above the ground. Every day, the arc grows wider and higher." He walked her around so she was facing north, his hand still pointing up, "Until the sun's all the way over here, over the ocean. Happens every year, just like calendar-work."

"There's no such word."

"Maybe not in English," he said, and winked.

They walked toward the aroma of yeast and oregano. "Do you want pizza? It's been a long time since I've eaten."

"Okay, but you're buyin'. I spent most of my money on chili and chips."

"I can do that. Do you want to eat in or take it back to Grandma's house?"

X couldn't contain her grin. "You're such a gentleman for asking. Let's take it back to Grandma's but ask for napkins so we don't have to wash any dishes. I didn't see a dog at your house and I don't think Q hires Fish Face out as a dishwasher."

"We do have water at the house for cooking, cleaning, and drinking, but we have to get it from the washeteria. That's another experience all together. You may have to check it out soon if your luggage doesn't show up."

X fingered the kuspuk, pulling it away from her tee shirt-covered belly. "For now, this works great and I don't miss wearing a bra. Actually, I think I could get used to wearing kuspuks. I might have to do something about another set of pants, though."

"Why?" Rocky asked, his mischievous grin making his dark brown eyes sparkle. He leaned into her hair and asked, "Don't you like getting into my pants?"

"Rocky!" she squealed. "Are you the same blushing man I met yesterday?"

He stepped back and gave her a puzzled look. "No," he said. "That was before I had you in my life. You're right, though. Blushing or not, I don't feel like the same man. I feel whole, complete. Do you know what I mean?"

X moved closer, into his arm that had opened out when he saw her intent. "Yes, I know exactly what you mean because I feel it, too."

"Kismet?" he asked.

"I don't know, but whatever it is, I like it!"

"Me, too. But right now, I'm ready for calories. Pick your topping, then we can wait on the deck while they bake it. I'd say watch the sunset, but that'd take too long."

"Pepperoni's fine with me," she said.

"How about reindeer sausage instead?"

X couldn't help but wrinkle her nose, then realized that Rocky wouldn't have suggested it if it was too extreme for her tastes. After all, he had watched out for her with the Eskimo ice cream and berries at bingo the night before. "What the heck; I'll try it."

Twenty minutes of gull and tern watching later, the pair were on their way back to the house, both quiet in apprehension. Where did they to go from here?

Rocky had shared his feelings with her—sort of—but would he just be a summer fling to her? A boy toy she'd toss aside and maybe remember twenty years later? Besides, where would she be in a month when he was in the army? He only had two weeks left before he had to report to Anchorage. He couldn't take her with him, and leaving her here with Grandma might be okay for the summer, but how would she handle the cold and darkness of winter? She'd need money, and from what she had said, she didn't have much for savings. It was doubtful her mother would help her out if she stayed in Alaska, a remote site full of 'not proper people,' totally unsuitable for a college graduate of her breeding. There weren't any paying jobs for archaeologists in Barrow. Besides, she'd probably starve if she lived on canned chili and evaporated milk.

X saw the scowl on Rocky's face as he pondered their future. She'd change his frown into a full smile of satiation after they'd eaten and had a little one-on-one time. Hopefully, Grandma had popped in and retrieved all the 'just one more things' she needed for her extended honeymoon with Joe.

Rocky opened the door for her, then stepped aside to let her in first. "Watch your step!"

"This time and every time for as long as I cross this threshold," she said, taking an exaggerated step down onto the mud mat in front of the door. "Looks like we're alone again."

"At least, for now," he said and set the pizza on the kitchen table.

X pulled the paper napkins from the restaurant out of her kuspuk pouch and set them on the table. "These pockets are sure handy. I've seen sweatshirts like these. I think they call them hoodies."

"They'll probably catch on. Front pockets are convenient for storing goods and for keeping your hands warm. Of course," he pulled a piece of pizza out of the box and handed it to her along with a napkin, "holding hot—or still mostly warm—pizza is good for that, too."

X looked at the sliced meat on the cheese-and-sauced flat bread. "It looks like pepperoni. I thought you said reindeer sausage."

"Pepperoni is a sausage, too. This is made from caribou, not beef or pork. Just as spicy, but better for you. Not as fatty."

X sampled a piece of the reddish-brown meat and smiled at the taste. "Wow! I could get used to eating this!" She took a full bite of the pizza and chewed thoroughly, watching him take his slice.

He took a big bite and let out an unintentional groan of satisfaction.

"Been a long time since you ate, huh?"

Rocky nodded and swallowed his bite. "Between you and Little Ben, it's been a long twenty-four hours."

They both ate their first pieces quickly, then paced themselves on the second ones. "I like cold pizza for breakfast, so I think I'll hold myself to two pieces."

Rocky handed her the bottle of water they were sharing and closed the box. "If you don't mind, I'd like to help you at the dig tomorrow. I don't think it can be too complicated, plus I don't trust Dr. Jackson. He might try something if you're alone with him. If you slapped him—and I don't doubt that you would if you were provoked—you could break open your stitches."

"I'd appreciate the help. I can't believe the gall of that man. And someone in the grant department okayed the hotel reservations for only two days for me. I don't know whether to be angry because they thought I'd quit that soon or pissed that they thought I was easy and their golden boy professor would be able to have his way with me in only two days."

"You won't have to worry about him with me around. I'm not a fighter, but I can get in the way of a forward pass. Just ask the basketball team."

"If you're not a fighter, does that mean you're a lover?" X

asked, eyes smiling, her grin stifled, but her dimples deep.

Rocky picked up the bottle of water and looked at her. He leaned in close, his mouth near her ear. "It means I'm not a fighter," he whispered, then pulled back. He opened the box and put his third piece of pizza back in it. Her hair had tickled his nose and the sensation of her nearness was now more important than food.

X stood up and looked down at him and saw he was blushing again. She hooked her index finger, indicating she wanted to tell him a secret, too. He stood up and inched next to her, his face still red. His teasing flirt had backfired on him and he had embarrassed himself, not her.

She put her uninjured hand on his shoulder and pulled him lower, so that now her face was close to the side of his head. She rubbed her nose around the outside of his ear, then whispered, "I can teach you to be a lover if you'll let me."

He stood up straight, grinned, and asked, "Experienced teacher?"

She shook her head, then repeated her hooked finger entreaty for him to lean down again. "How about we learn together?"

Rocky turned his head toward her and asked softly, "And

risk besmirching your integrity?"

She chuckled. "There you go again with those big town words. You were the one who told me the folks around here have their own lives to think about."

Rocky glanced at the door, for the first time in his life wishing the front door had a lock. Hopefully, Joe was keeping Grandma busy. "How about if I only dusty up your reputation a bit. Not that anyone would find out..."

"Be careful," she said, reaching up to stroke the side of his face. "I just might muddy up yours a little at the same time." She turned away and sauntered into the bedroom, and stopped beside the bed, her back to the doorway. Hopefully, Rocky was behind her and hadn't decided he needed to protect her virtue.

The thump of the refrigerator door shutting was followed by his footfalls as he approached the bedroom. Goosebumps raced from the back of her knees to her earlobes when she felt his nearness—his warmth but not his touch—as he stood behind her.

"Maybe just a little dust," he whispered in her ear.

She turned and crooned, "Uh, uh. I'm ready for a mud bath," then found his mouth with hers. As her kisses deepened, he responded, ready to commit to her, motivated by raging hormones, not common sense, the urge to breed stronger than his love and respect for the person.

She reached down with her good hand and unzipped the pants she had borrowed from him and shimmied out of them as her lips slid down his neck, pausing at the sweet soft point between his collar bones at the base of his neck, finally able to kick off the pants completely, the suction of her mouth keeping her upright.

On tiptoes now, she lifted one leg and wrapped it around his hip. Rocky reached down and pulled her closer, his hand slipping up her thigh until he reached her backside and realized she wasn't wearing panties.

He wanted to tell her to slow down, that at this pace they would soon get to a point where he wouldn't be able to stop himself. He'd done that once and swore he'd never let himself go with another woman until he knew for sure that she was the one.

"Alexandra Oppenheimer! What do you think you're doing? Don't you ever go all the way with a man unless you're married to him. Make him want you, treat you to all the nicest restaurants in the city, shower you with gifts.

Remember the old saying, 'Why buy the cow when you can get the milk for free?' Stop acting like a dairy!"

It had only been one time and she'd been caught the morning after. She should have thrown the panties in the trash before they left the park but hadn't thought of it. "What were you doing with that Collins boy last night?" her mother screeched, holding her blood-spotted panties in her hand. "You lost your virginity last night, didn't you? And with a store manager's son? If you're going to spread your legs, sweetie, at least choose someone with some status like a lawyer or judge's son. At least there we can claim you're pregnant and you can elope. Or better yet, get some hush money and then have a…ahem…miscarriage or abortion. Worked for me. Three times!"

That had been the summer before she started her sophomore year of college. She was never so eager to get back to classes. The tsk-tsking and head-shaking her mother shamed her with at least once daily almost made her run away from home. She didn't have anywhere to go, though. She didn't know where her grandmother lived, and she'd been told her father had died when she was a baby. However, the older she got and the more aware she became *of her mother's true personality, it wouldn't have surprised her if her father had run away!*

"Do you think we should slow down?" X panted, her inner conflicts raging, her mother's guilt-whipping winning out over her passion.

Rocky groaned softly as he released his clutch on her bottom, the loss of contact between their bodies a cold, achy void in his chest and in his loins. "Depends on which head I'm thinking with," he said, and chuckled nervously. "I think I'd better listen to this one," he said and tapped his temple. "Let's lie down and recover a minute."

They lay on their sides, face-to-face, her bandaged hand on his upper arm as he traced the line of her jaw with his finger. "You're so perfect," he whispered.

She chuffed briefly and half-smiled nervously. "You must have forgotten about my flat chest and patchwork belly. My face may not be scarred, but I'm far from perfect."

Rocky's hand drifted down the sleeve of her kuspuk to the hem of the overdress. He pulled it up to her hip and said, "Lie back."

X rolled onto her back as he gently tugged her kuspuk up, exposing her belly and more. He reached over and grabbed the scarf he had covered her chest with during the surgery and placed it lower as a modesty cover. "I really should check the sutures," he said. "Besides, maybe if I see that you're still healing, it will calm down my excitement."

X's eyes looked at the bulge in his pants. "I don't think so," she whispered, then looked toward her belly, "but I can't see what you're seeing, either."

Rocky pulled the dress back in place, then got out of bed and went to the window.

"What…where are you going?" she asked.

He removed two of the brown paper grocery bags from the top window panes. "I'm getting more light in here so I can see if there's any infection started." He reached down and rearranged himself. "And getting more comfortable. Those windows are high enough that no one can look inside."

X lifted her bottom and tugged her dress and undershirt up so he would have better access to her body, then quickly cupped her hand in front of her mouth, huffed, and checked her breath again. Pizza. At least they both tasted the same.

Rather than sit on the stool as he should have for a better view, Rocky knelt beside the bed. He felt as if he was worshipping her body, not examining it. He leaned forward and looked at each stitch in the first wound, his finger gliding next to each one to feel for swelling, then moved to the next one. He realized that her back was arching toward him at his touch. He stopped his examination. "Are you purring?" he asked.

Her back relaxed into the softness of the bed at the loss of his touch. "I suppose I was. I didn't realize it until you said something. I wasn't doing it on purpose."

Rocky resumed his visual and tactile inspection of her last and longest wound, her murmurs of contentment resuming at his touch, ceasing when he pulled his hand away.

"Do you have to stop?" she asked. "Can't you look for something else? Maybe there are some glass slivers you missed? You did say they might pop out later. It might be easier for you if I took off the kuspuk and the shirt. I'll need your help, though."

Rocky inhaled deeply, the request by a woman—his ideal woman—to be naked before him was almost too much for him to consider rationally.

Inspecting for glass shards with the kuspuk and tee shirt on or off—which would be easier to conduct and more conclusive? If she was in a doctor's office, he'd have her strip and put on a gown, not work around her day clothes. Think! Think with a physician's mind, not a lover's!

"Yes, it'd be best if you took off your clothes." He saw her begin to toss the first item aside, and rephrased his decision, "Yes on the everything else, but leave the scarf."

She set it back with a, "Hmph" of frustration, then reached out and let him help her sit up.

He pulled her clothes off over her head, shook them out, then folded and set them on the stool in the corner. He knelt back down beside her, ready for the examination, a mix of lust and fear giving him goosebumps that matched hers in size.

"I don't think it's fair that I'm mostly naked and you aren't," X said, licking her bottom lip then biting it, hoping she wasn't being too slutty. She sniffed back her embarrassment, then straightened her back, her resolve to be with him suddenly shameless. Fearless. Determined.

He set his forehead down on her thigh and closed his eyes, sighing in frustration that was so intense, he was afraid he'd wind up in tears. Should he give in to his lust and ruin what could be theirs for more than an afternoon or a few days, or hold off and see if she was willing to wait for now but be with him for the rest of their lives? He kissed her thigh, realizing the answer to his question was in his question.

"I can take off my shirt so you can touch my back and arms, but the pants stay on. If we're meant to be together, our feelings for each other will still be as strong tomorrow, next week, or next month as they are right now. I don't want to be like the Russian trappers who came to this area, found a moment of passion with a few of the women, then left them, ripping out their hearts, maybe leaving them with a small person to bring into the world, but with no man to take care of them or their children."

"But you don't have to worry about that with me…"

Rocky put up his hand, hovering it near her mouth without touching it. "I know, because we're not going to do anything that would make a baby."

"Sounds like you've already made up your mind," X said dejectedly.

He gently traced the invisible line that ran from her belly button up to the soft spot at the base of her throat. "I will check you for bits of glass, and I promise to make it as enjoyable as possible. I'll do it as a lover, not a doctor. Deal?"

he asked, then detoured down and to the right, creating a circle of sensation around the perimeter of her breast with the light touch of his finger.

Her back arched and her nipple hardened at the tease. "I don't know if I can let you do that all night long without attacking you or needing to be restrained, but I'll take all you can give me."

"Deal, then?"

"It's a deal," she purred and relaxed into the bed, ready for her lover's touch.

Chapter 7

"He said to meet him here at first light or eight o'clock. We left the house at twenty 'til and have been here for," X looked up at the sky and pretended to gauge the time by using hand-widths to mark the sun's position, "at least an hour."

"I think that's him coming now," Rocky said. "At least, that's Fran and her black Cadillac taxi."

"Huh?"

"The only taxi in town. At least, it's black under all the mud."

Rocky stepped forward, his hand extended to greet the man wearing a scowl, mirrored-sunglasses, and a new fur-hooded nylon parka.

Dr. Jackson glanced at Rocky, then looked away and walked past him with open arms to greet his personally picked intern, Alexandra Oppenheimer, the best-looking woman in the archaeology program.

"Ms. Oppenheimer! How good to see you!"

His attempt at a hug was thwarted as X quickly stepped

aside, instinctively moving close to Rocky.

Dr. J. winced at the slight, then realized he had a whole two months to win her over. "I hope you don't mind if I call you Alexandra—or maybe Alex—since we're going to be working so closely."

"Ms. Oppenheimer will work just fine," she said coolly. "I take it you didn't have any trouble finding the site?"

"Oh, no. That lovely lady—Ann, I believe she said—took me on a tour of the city. Or village. It really is quite quaint. Did you know that most of these homes don't have running water or flushing toilets?"

"Yes, as a matter of fact, I did know that. And did you know that plumbing hasn't kept these people from thriving in one of the most hostile environments in the world? I wonder, do you think you or anyone else at the university could survive one winter, much less generations, up here without electricity?"

Dr. Jackson snorted at what he perceived as an intentional insult to his intelligence. "Well, I could if my parents had taught me what to do!"

"Well, maybe," she said, "but somewhere along the way, that parent's parent's parent had to figure out how to keep warm and fed." She looked over at Rocky and smiled. "And I think you missed saying hello to my friend and assistant."

X held up her bandaged hand. "I had a little accident. Sergei Rachmaninoff has offered to help me out."

"Ah, a Russky got a little frisky with grandma, eh?" the professor snipped.

"I don't think my grandmother would appreciate that comment, sir," Rocky said and stuffed his hands in his front pockets, making sure the arrogant man of letters knew he didn't want to shake his hand. He had offered once and been snubbed. The second introduction had ended in a slur against his family. Hopefully, this overeducated boor would tire of the terrain and mosquitoes in a hurry and go back to the elitist circle he had come from.

"I don't know if *Ms. Oppenheimer,*" Dr. Jackson looked to X when he said her name and winked, "instructed you on our procedures, so I'll go over them again."

Rocky's jaw clenched every time the senior archaeologist got close to X, rubbing up against her—or trying to—as he illustrated basic digging and sifting, and how he wanted the gridded area documented and photographed. When X almost tripped a second time trying to elude his pawing, Rocky stepped in between them.

"Sir, Ms. Oppenheimer sustained more injuries than are visible. If she falls, she could reinjure herself and be hospitalized. I suggest you give her a wide berth."

"Who are you," the professor snarled, "her doctor?"

"As a matter of fact," X piped in, "he is."

"Where'd he get his diploma? The School of Hard Knocks?"

"My physician's accreditation is not your concern," X said. "You're here to supervise the dig. I'm here to assist and get experience. Now, I didn't plan to get hurt, and I spent the majority of my savings to get here, so if this skilled person who has volunteered his valuable time to assist me as I direct him on where to dig and what to catalogue won't work out for you, then tell me now. I'm sure Scotty would be more than happy to buy a last-minute ticket to Alaska and buddy up with you on this project."

Rocky stood back, his arms crossed in front of his chest while the man rightfully called Dr. Jackass took his dressing down, the arrogant man's close-shaven cheeks scarlet at being told off by a twenty-one-year-old female intern.

"Well, it looks like you went and picked up an attitude

along with that ratty old Native dress you're wearing," he snipped, then turned around and realized he had nowhere to go. He hadn't been paying attention on the ride in and was disoriented. He knew the hotel was nearby but didn't know where. He had a cellphone, but there was no service up here. He was stuck and at the mercy of an impertinent and soon-to-be discharged intern and her Native boyfriend.

"The hotel's that way," Rocky said, pointing down the road. "Be careful not to get mud on your new shoes. We backwards Natives haven't figured out how to pave the roads yet."

"So I see," Dr. Jackson scoffed. "I'll be back after lunch to see how you two are coming along. Try to get a better attitude or you, *Ms. Oppenheimer*, may have to make another career choice. In order to get an endorsement from me with regards to archaeology, you have to be a team player."

X walked up to Rocky and threaded her arm through his, holding him close. The two watched as the clumsy professor—his nose literally held high in the air—stumbled, tripped up by the occasional loose stones on the hard-packed gravel road.

"Why don't they pave the roads?" she asked, her head now against his shoulder.

"Perma-frost. It's better this way. You don't want to trap the heat in the roadbed and melt the permafrost underneath it. It's better to keep it cold and even." He reached around and patted her other shoulder, stopping short of a full hug in case the professor turned around. "You're right. Dr. Jackass does fit him better."

"Yeah, and by 'team player,' he was saying I'd never get anywhere unless I slept with him. Since he's tenured and I'm just a graduate in need of experience, looks like I'm either going to have to find another college to be associated with or change career paths."

Rocky chuckled. "That's my girl."

"What do you mean?"

"You didn't even consider sleeping with the man to get ahead."

"Ew! I'd rather clean toilets—or honey buckets—for a living. Come to think of it, though… Remember when we were talking about my mother?"

"I remember when you told me about her."

"Yeah. Anyhow, she's the one who wanted to be an

archaeologist. She had the hots for the actor in those movies. I don't know if she thought I'd be bringing home Harrison Ford or golden icons, but either way, it was her dream, not mine. I'd rather help heal people—like you do—than dig dry bones."

"It's never too late to go back to school. Even if you worked as an aide until you could get a new set of letters after your name, you'd be helping real people..."

"Instead of placating lettered philanderers."

They both laughed.

"There we go again," Rocky said.

"Finishing each other's sentences," X added.

"And lovin' it."

"Ready to dig in to see if we can find great-grandma's dishes?" X asked.

"Just show me where. Oh, and by the way, Q told me that the potlatch Grandma was trying to put together was for the young woman they found here."

"Better to have her funeral late than never, I suppose. Come on, my remote-controlled hands, we'll start over here. I doubt I'll continue this career path, but I hate to leave a job undone. Besides, this is for great-great-grandma and your village, not Dr. Jackass."

"Amen to that!"

***

"How about some soup for dinner," Rocky asked as they approached the house, arm-in-arm.

"I was hoping for something besides pizza. It was good, but it got old after having it for breakfast and lunch, too. Even if we hadn't eaten it all, I don't think I could handle another bite."

"I have some potatoes, onions, and frozen fish. I can make some chowder."

"I'll contribute my can of condensed milk. Since they still haven't found my luggage, I don't have my fancy tea. I guess I don't need it, huh?"

Rocky looked down at the rolled-up cuffs on the borrowed corduroy slacks and mended kuspuk. "Looks like you've gone Native to me. It looks good on you."

"I know winter is rough, but it's the people who make a town—or in this case, a village—a great place to live. I mean, where else can you walk to the beach to go to work, have your boyfriend at your beck and call, doing everything you ask, and then he still volunteers to make dinner for you?"

130

Rocky tugged her close and whispered, "You forgot to say where you also have your own personal physician."

X whispered back, "Can we play doctor while the soup's cooking? I'll help you peel the potatoes…" She looked down at her hand, still held close to her chest in a makeshift calico-rag sling. "I guess not this time. Shoot! What can I do?"

"I'd say supervise, but the kitchen is one place where I don't need help. Don't worry about it. One of these days, I might need an extra hand, too."

"I certainly hope not, for your sake, but if you do, just call."

Rocky smiled weakly at her comment. It probably wouldn't be from the next room but would have to be a long-distance call. He sniffed back his uncertainty, willing himself to enjoy life in the moment. She was a wonderful woman, but would she be willing to wait for his three-year enlistment term to end?

Rocky opened the front door and X nearly tripped again when she walked in.

"Whoa!" he hollered, grabbing her elbow from behind to keep her on her feet. "What happened?"

"My suitcase! Someone brought my suitcase to your

house." She grabbed it by the handle and slid it out of the way. "And whoever it was set it right in the doorway, so I'd be sure to see it. Hey, how'd they know I was staying here?"

"I told you, everyone knows everyone in this town. You should be flattered."

"Why?"

"Someone believes you're one of us," he said, eyebrows raised. "You even look like a Native."

"Thanks! Now, let's see how I handle fish stew. If it's anything like clam chowder, I'm all for it."

Rocky carried the suitcase into the bedroom and opened it for her, then went back in the kitchen and got dinner started. When he came back in, X was seated on the stool, her head in her hand. He put his hand on her shoulder, "What's wrong?"

"I can't believe how much junk I have. I don't need any of this. I've wasted so much of my life and money of accumulating worthless crap. Or high-priced stuff that I do need but that doesn't need to be so frilly or padded." She held up three fancy bras. "Do you need some packing material?"

"Depends on if I need to box up a few of Grandma's

glass fishing floats," he said. "Nah, you don't need those. I like the way you're built. You have all the right parts." He pulled her up next to him, then put his hands under her arms on either side of her petite breasts. "Gorgeous milk jugs, whether they're empty or full, pint-sized or gallon. Plus, the dispensers are fun to play with, even when they're empty."

X grinned and blushed, despite herself. "How long until dinner?" she asked and winked.

He looked down at his watch. "Only fifteen minutes until I need to check the potatoes. I set the timer just in case we got carried away. Or I can help you unpack and clear the bed for after dinner. We won't be interrupted then."

"Unless Grandma comes back. Maybe she'll want these?" X twirled the bra straps around her finger.

"Double-barreled slingshots," Rocky said, then took them from her and set them on the dresser. He leaned down and kissed her on the side of the neck, murmuring as he made his way to the crook near her shoulder, "I'm going to be greedy and take an aperitif *and* dessert."

***

The second day on the site was difficult. X was feeling better and couldn't resist the temptation to reach out and help. Finally, Rocky pulled her away and set her hand back in the sling. "Stay! Direct only."

"But you don't know what to do…"

"I said, direct only. Use your words," he said, frowning in frustration.

"But it looks like it's going to rain. I don't want to give Dr. Jackass a reason to blame me for not getting this done on time…"

"And I'm running out of bandages. Let's try to keep it at one re-wrap a day, okay?"

"Yes, doctor. Whatever you say," X said, her grin containing the boisterous laugh she wanted to share.

Rocky shook his head in exasperation. "If you want a high-dollar physician, try the clinic. Right now, I'm probably the best you can afford."

"Oh, I'm sorry," she said, her sudden humiliation causing her stomach to roil. "I appreciate all you do for me. Really, I do. I'm just so used to having everything a certain way. At least, on a small scale. I guess I've been my mother's puppet for so long, that I expected to be a puppet master when I grew up, too. Forgive me?"

"Sure," Rocky said, and bent back to his task, certain

that in a few minutes, she'd revert to the same bossy person.

"I'm serious, Rocky. Let me know—gently—if I cross the line. Maybe just a throat-clearing. I'll take the hint. Promise."

"Okay. I believe you. Nome wasn't built in a day and building a truly coordinated archaeological team takes time, too, I'm sure."

"I'll work on your team any day, Doc."

"Back at ya, Captain."

***

"The clerk at the hotel and Oscar and Lisa mentioned the red raven and looked at me. What's going on with that?"

"I think you've already figured out that I mildly detest alcohol and drinking…"

"Mildly and detest don't go together," X said, then ran a finger down his belly, stopping short of the area he had designated as off limits. She brought it back up again and said, "Maybe mildly disgusted or absolutely detest…"

Rocky inhaled deeply at her provocative tickle and gasped, "The second one," and took her hand and held it close to his heart. "If I'm going to tell you the story, you have to stop interrupting and distracting me."

"Yes, dear," she giggled, and snuggled into his upper

arm.

"So, the reason I don't *care* for alcohol is no good ever comes of it. When I was only sixteen, Q and I were at a friend's uncle's house. He invited us to have a drink. I knew what happened to others when they drank, but I thought I was different, that I'd be able to enjoy the taste and then go on my way. Nope. It tasted horrible! He used that brown mouthwash as a base for the liquor, then added crushed berries and I don't know what else. They were just going for the effect. I think the berries were to make it look like wine. Of course, when I said that was not for me, they insisted that it always tasted better after the first few swallows. It did because I had no tolerance for the stuff.

"Pretty soon, we were all bragging about our conquests, telling secrets to one up each other, or maybe they were lies. I don't know because I don't remember. It was winter and it was only by the grace of God that I made it home. I couldn't get the door open when I got to Grandma's. There isn't even a lock on the door, but I couldn't figure out how to turn the handle. She heard the thunk as I fell against the door and dragged me in. She never said a word, just held my head over the bucket while I puked 'til I passed out. When I kept puking when I was unconscious, she stayed awake with me so I didn't aspirate vomit and suffocate.

"Anyhow, two days later, the guys started teasing me, asking me if I'd found my red raven yet. I knew about my dream, about growing old with the red-haired woman who was my mate for life, but I didn't know how they knew. I didn't remember telling them. And then I realized: I had shared my most treasured image with a bunch of drunks. Yes, they were my friends, but they didn't treat my vision as the sacred trust it was."

"You didn't act upset when Oscar or the clerk asked about it."

"I wasn't. They knew how important my vision was. They weren't teasing me; they were hoping it was true. There's a big difference."

"So, am I your Red Raven?"

"I don't know yet. We're not old, and I haven't had the trials I know I need to go through. I want you to be, but there's no way you can force a vision to come true."

***

Ten days passed with Rocky assisting X at the dig. He had taken the stitches out of her hand and belly after a week, but insisted she keep her hand out of the dirt. The lightweight gauze bandaging he used allowed her the freedom to photograph objects found and record the notations and measurements while Rocky did the excavating and cleaning.

"You know I could probably do this by myself if I had to," X said, then realized what her day would be like without Rocky in it. "But I'm not ready to try. I mean… Am I still in danger of infection or something?"

Rocky wiped the dirt from his hands on a rag and came to sit down beside her on the other camp chair. He picked up the water bottle and took a long drink, searching for an honest answer that didn't sound too sappy. "We're always in danger of something. We can't go through life scared. But I'd rather spend my days with you, digging in the dirt as your warm-blooded excavator, than down at the center, waiting for calls to come in. Besides, whaling doesn't start for a couple months. It'll be plenty busy then. For now, I'll take life one day at a time."

A cold chill ran up her back as she realized the two of them had no real commitment. One day at a time used to sound great, but what she wanted from him was a forever.

"Yeah, one day at a time," she echoed, her eyes wide in fear.

"For now," Rocky repeated and kissed her on the cheek. "I'm not a quitter."

X picked up her pen and waved it like a light saber, adding a feigned smile to cover the sudden nausea that had settled in the pit of her stomach. "Me, either."

***

Each day, Dr. Jackson showed up around four in the afternoon, noted her progress in his journal, and asked redundant questions, the answers already entered in her detailed daily reports.

"He knows we're doing a great job," X told Rocky, "but he wouldn't say so if his job depended on it, which it doesn't. As a class project this spring, we determined a timeline for the excavation based on the preliminary reports given to us by the borough. I'm more than a week ahead of schedule."

"Must be due to the diligence of your assistant," Rocky said, then smiled and winked.

"You know, every time you wink at me like that," she

139

said, "I feel like you're throwing me a kiss."

"I guess I'm doing it right then," he said and winked again.

On the eleventh day, Dr. Jackson came out. "*Ms. Oppenheimer,*" he said icily, "I'm leaving you here unsupervised. I'll be attending a seminar in California. I suggest you not take my absence as an excuse to slack in your responsibilities and decide to spend more time…ahem…entertaining the locals. I'll be back when you least expect it. I have everything documented and know how much has been accomplished and how much still needs to be finished before the season ends. Your reputation in the field depends on my report, so don't screw up."

Rocky watched X's jaw muscles twitch as she decided whether to tell Jackson off or submit to her designated supervisor. Common sense won out. Her only reply was a nod that she had heard him.

"Why, yes, thank you very much, Ms. Oppenheimer," Dr. Jackson said snidely. "I'm sure I'll have a good time. The California beaches in July are so much nicer—and sunnier—than Barrow's. Oh, and I'll be sure to use plenty of sunscreen, especially since I'll be spending part of my time at one of the most renowned and exclusive nude beaches."

Dr. Jackson finished his sarcastic soliloquy, then looked over at Rocky and sneered.

"Might want to take some bug spray with you, too," Rocky said and grinned. "I hear sand flea bites will swell to three or four times their size. Then again, in your case, that might work to your benefit on a nude beach."

"Hmph!" the professor snorted, and turned and stomped away, headed toward his sanctuary, the king-sized hotel room that was still not big enough to hold all his rage and frustration.

"What's that?" X whispered to Rocky as she watched the angry man stumble one more time, something white trailing behind him.

Rocky followed her finger and chuckled. "Looks like a toilet paper tail to me," he said.

"I think you're right. I sure hope it's one of the locals who bring it to his attention. He's such a high and mighty bigot."

"Actually, I prefer to think of bigots as low and slimy. They just *think* they're superior to everyone else," Rocky said.

"And by that one belief alone, prove that they are

beneath the masses," X said, finishing his thought.

Chapter 8

"Why do you always stop me? I know you want me—at least, I'm pretty sure you do. I know I certainly want you! Is there something wrong?"

Rocky shook his head.

"Are you scared?"

Once again, Rocky shook his head, this time, adding a scowl at being hounded.

When she didn't get an audible answer, she whispered, "Are you a virgin?"

"No."

"That's it? No, you're not a virgin?" she asked.

"Yes."

"Huh?"

"Would you want the store manager's son to tell about his little fling with you?"

"No, I guess not, but it's different when its's from your perspective. Did something happen that you're afraid to tell me? Did she have your baby?" X asked, suddenly insecure about her position in who was the most precious person in his life.

Rocky squinted at her and shook his head, then groaned and laughed at the same time. "I guess I'd better tell you or you'll be more miserable than I was. It was only once. She was older than I was and, shall we say, very experienced." He shrugged. "She laughed at me."

"What? Unless you painted a clown face on your dick, I don't see why she'd laugh at you."

"At first she giggled because I didn't have a condom in my wallet like all the other guys who came to see her did. She had me pick one out of the assortment she kept in her purse." Rocky huffed, his face red, recalling the embarrassment. "Then she laughed out loud when she saw I didn't know how to put it on."

X's stomach churned as she shared his humiliation on a gut level. She kissed his hand, letting him know she understood, then rolled onto her back and bared her belly. "You don't have to worry about condoms with me. You couldn't give me a baby if you tried. I can't have one. I'm sure you saw the old scars on my belly when you were sewing me up."

She elbowed herself half-way up and traced the jagged

scars just above her pelvis. "They're from a car accident. I was all messed up on the inside, parts of the other guy's car half-embedded in my body. I was only twelve, but I overheard the doctor tell my mother that I'd never be able to have a baby. She about freaked out. I thought she was concerned about me, then I heard her tell him he'd better not put that in any of his reports or she'd tell his wife about their affair. When he said he'd never messed around with anyone, including her, she said, 'I know that, but she doesn't.' She wanted me to find the best—and by the best, I mean the richest—husband possible on the east coast. If it was known I was sterile, it would be a deal-breaker for about half the prime contenders."

She leaned back and sighed, sad and relieved that she had shared her humiliation and shame: she was barren. He knew everything there was to know about her now: all the evils of her family, her body, her secrets, her fears. He'd either accept her or reject her. All the love and hope that she had to offer was out there for him to nurture and adore, or toss into the lagoon, like a honey bucket of human waste.

His warm breath on her neck sent goosebumps all the way to the soles of her feet, if that was even possible. Her toes curled in response. "Joining with you would be the end of one life and the beginning of another. Making a child is not what I mean by that, either. I made a mistake once with having intercourse with a woman I didn't love. I was too young to know what I was doing. That's my only valid excuse and the reason I didn't go crazy. I gave her something I can never have back. I'm not talking about my virginity, either. I gave her a part of me, not just physically, but spiritually. At that moment, when two become one, it's either something wonderful that's created, or one person is taking from the other. I was nothing but a whoopie for her, a diversion, a heightened sensation similar to what she could get from marijuana or alcohol. She used me."

"And what we have here…" X asked, insecurity racing across her chest, binding her breathing with steel wires of doubt. "We're just sharing sensations, too. Is that what you're saying—getting drunk on hormonal stimulations?"

"No!" Rocky quickly turned to her and held her close, her bare chest to his, the feel of her skin chilled in fear even more heartbreaking because he knew he had caused it. "What we have is different. I don't know how to explain it, but if you were anyone but who you are, I wouldn't be here."

"Rocky, I want to grow old with you." X reached up and ran her fingers through the thick dark hair on the top of his head. "Even if you lose all these luscious locks and get fat and even more ornery, I still want to be in your life."

"As the village archaeologist?" he teased.

"As your wife."

"The pay would suck."

X stroked up and over the bulge in his pants, teasing the zipper with her fingernail, knowing that the rumble over the metal teeth sent tiny vibrations to the man trapped beneath. "Yes, but the benefits would be phenomenal."

"Or so you hope…" Rocky nudged his nose across her bottom lip, following it as she gasped, her hands stilled with his distraction.

He pulled back, letting her recover her breath, hoping she'd get back to teasing the zipper again. *Maybe today…*

"Grandma told me about finding that special someone one day. I think she found hers in Joe. She did say he was the one she married years ago. Partners have come and gone in both their lives, but they still wind up with each other. Even alcohol couldn't break them apart."

"Well, it did separate them for a while a couple dozen

times," Rocky said, then added dryly, "At least. But you're right. I want what they have, but without the booze or breaks. I want to be mated for life."

"Like the swans?"

"Lots of animals are like that. Man and woman should be, too."

"Rocky, are you ready to mate for life? With me?"

"I don't know…"

Rocky saw her fear and amended his reply. "I don't know about now, but I do know it's you. No doubt in my mind."

"Mine, either. So, if it's forever, what are we waiting for? I've wanted you since… Well, I can't pinpoint the minute, but I do know it didn't even take 24 hours to know how special you were. It took a few more hours to realize that I didn't want to lose you. Shoot! And now, I even like the food around here."

"You don't have much choice, but you still haven't tried muktuk," he said, then kissed her neck.

"Only because there isn't any around yet. Just wait until they bring in the first bowhead. I'll show you that I'm not afraid of the unknown."

Rocky moved her hand back on his zipper. "Why don't

you show me now?"

X's eyes widened. "You're not talking about muktuk, are you?"

A groan escaped as Rocky arched his back, filling her hand. "Nope."

"Looks like you rose to the challenge first. Now it's my turn."

Zippp…

Chapter 9

X arched her back, not even trying to contain her groan of satisfaction. According to tradition—at least, the way she chose to believe it—she was now Mrs. Sergei Rachmaninoff. Even if the two of them didn't spend the rest of their lives in Barrow, they'd be together. Forever.

Mated for life.

"You know what I'd really like?" she said.

Rocky stretched and yawned, mimicking her guttural purr, then picked up her hand and kissed the faded spot on her left wrist where her watch had been, the digits M4L still penned in with marker. He traced the midline of her belly down to her pubic hair. "You name it. If it's mine to give, it's yours."

"Not that, silly," she said. "Maybe later, when I can put my legs together again."

"I think it's more fun when your legs are apart..." He started kissing her neck, working his way down, watching her nipples harden in anticipation of more wedded joining.

X giggled and shrugged her shoulder up, blockading his

attack. "What I'd really love is a cup of my fancy tea with a spoonful of sugar and a splash of canned milk."

"Hmm… I used the last of the milk, but I can run down and get a can from Q's store."

"You'd better put on some pants first. I wouldn't want you to make Q or the others feel bad," she said, then chuckled into her hand.

"I'm just average but running naked through town in July isn't a good idea, especially in the morning when mosquitoes are their hungriest."

"Honey, there's nothing average about you, not now and probably never was or will be. I'll get the water boiling while you make the milk run."

Rocky pulled his tee shirt on over his head, then bent down and kissed her upturned face. "I sure love you, Mrs. Rachmaninoff," he said, then stepped into his jeans. "As soon as you say the word, we can make it legal in the white man's world, too."

"Okay, but I want tea first."

"I'll be back in a flash." He paused at the door, slipped on his tennis shoes without socks, and sprinted to the store.

Rocky bent forward and caught his breath before he entered the store. "Hey, Q," he said when his cousin came in from the back of the store carrying a carton of pilot bread. "Can't chat now. Gotta get some milk for my lady's tea."

"Making a milk run—literally a run—for a woman you just met? Man, she's got you by the short hairs!"

"Yes, she does. And I'm not complaining, either." He set the can on the counter, pulled out his wallet, and gasped.

"What's wrong?" Q asked. "I was just joking…"

Rocky pulled the paper out of the dollar bill part of his wallet and looked again. "What day is it?"

"Sunday."

"I mean, what date is it?"

Q pointed to the poster-sized calendar covered with cans of various sodas. "July 10, all day long. Why?"

"Crap." He huffed in frustration, looked down where his watch should have been and saw the inked-in 'M4L' that was identical to the one on X's wrist. He looked up and saw the time on the big clock on the wall. "Is that the correct time?"

Q scowled as he looked at his cousin and best friend

again. "Yes. Are you all right?"

Rocky didn't have to ask what time the next flight to Anchorage was; everyone in town knew the schedules and when they changed. He had less than half an hour before the plane left. He could make it to the airport in time but didn't have time to go home and explain what was going on to X, too.

"Do you have a pen and paper?" he asked.

"Yeah, sure." Q pulled out the store's daily journal: a dog-eared spiral notebook. "Help yourself. Just don't tear out any pages with writing on them. I gotta finish unloading the truck. I finally have enough food to fill the shelves again!"

Rocky flipped through the pages, found a blank one, and wrote,

'Gotta jet! If I don't make this flight, they'll throw me in the brig. I can't call, but I'll write and explain everything. Stay at Grandma's while you finish the dig. You'll hear from me soon. M4L. Love, R'

He folded it in half several times, reached behind the counter and grabbed the tape dispenser, and sealed the note. "Take this to Grandma's and give it to X, would you?" he asked, waving the note in the air.

Q stumbled in with another box. "Yeah, sure, as soon as I get my shelves stocked."

"No. As soon as you're done unloading the truck, maybe. Don't make her wait. I gotta… I gotta go. I can't explain, but I'll write."

"Okay. But…"

"No time for buts," Rocky said, and slapped the note on the counter. "Don't forget!"

And then he was gone, sprinting to the airport to catch the flight to Anchorage so he fulfilled his contract of enlistment. The enlisting officer stressed that if he didn't show up, they'd find him and put him in prison. The man's eye twitched when he said it, and he could have been lying, but there's no way he wanted to find out the hard way that it was the truth. He and X could work around him being in the army for three years, but being AWOL and in the brig, his credit ruined, a criminal record… that was too much for starting their married life.

"Bye," Q whispered sarcastically, then went to the backdoor again, ready to load up the hand truck with the canned goods.

Dr. Jackson stepped out from behind the tall greeting

and post card carousel, made sure the clerk called Q was out of view, then grabbed the love note to his hot, inapproachable intern written by her sassy Native assistant. He read it then chuckled softly as he grabbed the notebook. "Time for a little payback, hotshot."

'I got a better offer. Go back to the hotel with Dr. Jackson. He'll take care of you. This would never have worked between us. R'

He quickly folded the note and hastily taped it closed before anyone caught him making the switch. He shoved the true note in his pocket just as Q walked in from the back with the boxes of canned foods.

"Can I help you, sir?"

"Just looking for a few postcards for my lady friends," the professor said, then randomly pulled half a dozen of them out of the rack without looking at them. "That'll be all." He slammed a five-dollar bill down on the table. "Keep the change," he added, then walked out with cards in hand, whistling in pride at his deception, then tossed the cards in the trash can by the door. "Payback's a bitch," he crooned, "and so are you."

"You just made it, sir. We called your name twice and were getting ready to seal the door. Don't you have any luggage or carryon?"

"Nope. Just me," he said, biting off the comment, 'And I'm not even wearing socks or underwear!'

***

X waited a full hour for Rocky to come back before she went to the store looking for him.

"Hey, Q," she called out when she saw him stocking the shelves. "Have you seen Rocky? He left the house an hour ago to get canned milk and hasn't been back."

"Oh, yeah," Q said, a blush of embarrassment rising as he remembered he was supposed to have given her the note earlier. "He said to give you this, and then he split. I mean, he really split. I knew he had some speed, but he four-minute-miled out of here. Hey, did you know he was captain of the basketball team? We won state regionals when he was in charge..."

X was only half-listening as Q babbled while she tried to unseal the note without destroying it. Rocky was usually so neat and orderly, but the note he had taped up looked like it had been done by a kindergartner. Finally, she took Q's box cutter from the counter and slit the tape so she didn't tear the paper. Her face paled as she read the words.

"No. No, no, no, no…" She looked at Q who had turned away from his stocking duties, more interested in the drama unfolding in front of him.

"No, what?" he asked.

"He didn't leave, did he?"

"Yeah, he did. After he verified today's date and the time, he scribbled that note and asked me to give it to you as soon as possible. Then he ran that way. If I didn't know better, I'd say he was catching the flight to Anchorage."

Chapter 10

July 18, 2016
Utqiaġvik (Barrow), Alaska

"What then, Mama?"

"I waited with Grandma for almost a week, working on the dig sixteen hours a day until I could get all I had contracted to do finished. Dr. Jackson tried his best to persuade me to stay with him, insisting the benefits far outweighed my prissy morals. Finally, after the fifth day and no word, I called my mother, asked to borrow enough money to get home—pretty much groveled away all the self-respect I'd managed to build with Rocky—and stayed with her for a whole two days."

"What happened then?" Krista asked.

"I found Grandma Lou's phone number written in an old organizer tucked in the back of her desk. I called her, chatted until I heard Mom come in from her shopping trip, then realized I managed better with grandmothers than mothers. Of course, I did my best not to burn bridges, but Mom started with her drama queen performance, said I was breaking her heart by leaving again, that she had found the most perfect man for me, but I had to go with her to the regatta in Timbuktu or somewhere to meet him... Anyhow, I told her I got an offer I couldn't refuse. I stuffed my ratty old kuspuk, a couple of tank tops, a spare pair of jeans and clean underwear in a backpack and I was gone—taking not much more than the clothes on my back and my reclaimed self-respect."

"What was the better offer?"

"Your great-grandmother said, 'Come as you are. I'll take care of you.' And that was that." X paused. "Well, sorta. A month later, my period hadn't started. I thought it was the stress, but at her insistence, I took a pregnancy test. Of course, I was all over the place with emotions: happy that I was going to have the baby I was told I'd never have; sad that I didn't have your father in my life to share the joy with; angry that he still hadn't contacted me..."

"Mom," Krista interrupted, her hand gentle on her mother's shoulder, trying to calm her down as she relived emotions twenty-two years old. "Did my father know how to contact you? Did you leave a phone number or address with

Grandma or Q? Did you even think to call Q at the store and find out what had happened?"

"No… So much for certified genius, eh?" X shook her head. "It didn't make a difference. At the time, my hurt was so intense, I couldn't focus. I also had to find a way to raise a child on my own. I had renewed sympathy for those Native women the whalers and fur trappers had cozied up to, left them pregnant and with no man to help them. I took some practical classes on health care, then transferred a bunch of my credits and got a head start on a nursing degree. Pediatrics called me at first—probably because I had you—but then I transitioned into care for the elderly. The money's not great, but the rewards emotionally are fantastic."

"Yeah, I know what you mean. When I see those old folks' faces light up when you enter the room, it makes *me* proud. And I'm just your daughter!"

"Krista, there's no 'just your daughter' when it comes to you. So, now you know. You're half Inupiaq, half crazy white woman."

"Mom! Mom!" Lars called as he ran up the hill. "Can I play basketball with these guys?"

"Go for it. Just be back to the hotel by…" She looked up

at the sky and squinted, pretending to gauge the time, and pointed. "By the time the sun gets there or five o'clock, whichever comes first."

Lars rolled his eyes at one of the oldest jokes in his mother's limited repertoire. "Okay, but if it's a tie game, I might be a little late. But don't worry. No one's going to kidnap me..."

"If you don't mind, Mama, I'm going to take a little walk by myself. No offense, but this is a lot to process. In one way I'm glad you didn't tell me when I was younger. No telling how I would have reacted." Krista kissed her mother on the cheek. "Yup, you're still a great mother. Oh, and as far as I'm concerned—even if it sounds less romantic or exotic—I'm not a love child. You were married—lousy divorce—but married when I was conceived."

X bit her bottom lip and waved her daughter good-bye. She needed a cry by herself. Why hadn't she seen all the signs? The note that was left couldn't have been written by Rocky—it was too messy. Plus, he would never, ever tell her to go stay with Dr. Jackass. That self-absorbed philanderer had to be behind all this.

X walked through town, looking for old landmarks,

checking out the new ones. A Chinese restaurant had come in, but the Mexican one had burned down. Q's Market was still there, but she wasn't brave enough to see if Q was still there. Or was she?

Before she knew it, she was in the store, bringing the cans forward and turning them so the labels were out, making the shelves look fuller than they really were. When she got to the chili, she checked the price. Still five bucks. Apparently, the cost of food in the Arctic north had caught up with inflation.

Woof! Woof!

X looked down and saw a black three-legged dog, his white muzzle and cloudy eyes verifying he was ancient. "Fish Face?" she asked.

"How'd you know my dog's name?" The teenage female clerk asked.

"Well, I'll be," said the gray-haired man who had come in from the back of the store to stand behind his daughter. "If it isn't Red Raven."

"Q?"

"We're having a special on chips and chili. Interested?"

"Do you have a microwave? That works?"

"Yes and no. Yes, we have a microwave, and no, this one doesn't work, either. I never thought I'd see you again. How're you doing?"

Unsure of how to answer his question X grinned, then grimaced, finally spared having to answer his question by her son bursting into the store.

"Mom! Mom! There you are," said Lars. "You gotta see this."

"Oh, okay." She turned to Q. "I'm not going anywhere for a few days. I'll be back after I check out what the excitement's all about. Oh, this is my son, Lars."

"Mo-om! Come on!" he said and tugged her elbow.

"Later," X said, then followed her son, half-running, half-walking to keep up with him.

"Ah, man!" Lars groaned. "He's gone. He was playing with us guys, spinning the ball on the end of his fingertip like a pro! And jump! He could jump and guard and shoot from the outside…"

"Yeah, and…?"

"He only had one foot! I mean, he had two, but one of them was chrome or aluminum or something like that. It looked weird, but it sure didn't slow him down."

"Hey, Lars. We need another guy. You wanna join us?"

Lars squinted up at the sky, pretending to tell the time. "Yeah, sure. I got a while still." He turned back to his mother. "Mom, I know I said I never wanted you to get married again, but I think I'd like him for a dad. He's cool!"

"Well, I'm glad you've got an open mind, son, but I'm not looking."

Lars turned to join his friends. "Just saying," he called back.

"Hey, Mom," Krista said, waving from across the street. "Stay put—I'll be right there." She looked both ways, waited for the four-wheeler loaded with baskets full of laundry to pass, then crossed the street to her mother. "I think I like small towns. At least, this one. No cell phones needed. Just go outside and look around and there you are. And Lars. I'm sure glad he's doing something besides going cross-eyed with his video games."

"You and me both. So, did you find anything interesting? A pick-up jam session maybe?"

Krista chuckled. "You know me too well. But as a matter of fact, I did. Come on over a couple of blocks. You're not going to believe this. A baby grand piano. It's practically as big as the whole house!"

X watched as her daughter told her story, Krista animated with her revelation, her hands talking louder than her mouth. "I heard classical music coming from this house, at full volume. It was so loud, I thought I was in an auditorium! I wanted to see what kind of speakers gave such clear tones. And when I got there, it was a little old lady on a baby grand piano, her fingers dancing across the keys, tickling out Variations on a Theme by Paganini."

"By Rachmaninoff."

"Yeah, that's the one. And when I stood in the doorway, waiting for her to finish so I could tell her how much I enjoyed her performance, she turned and called to me by name! Except she called me her granddaughter. 'Ah, my granddaughter, Krista! Welcome! I've been waiting for you!' It was kinda spooky, but…"

Krista stopped talking and reached out to grab her mother around the waist when she saw her knees buckle. "Are you okay, Mama?"

X's eyes widened as she looked up. The house didn't look the same. It was nearly twice the size it had been. It had to be in order to fit the piano. Someone had extended one side of the wooden structure and added bright yellow all-weather siding, the once unpainted exterior only a memory. The front yard was tidy, a decorative wheelbarrow loaded with almost a dozen glass fishing floats. She looked at the scar on her palm, faded white but still visible, the memories of intense pain and the pleasuring that happened soon afterwards a tumble of emotions that crowded out the real world.

"Mama, are you going to be okay?" Krista asked again, her hand now on her mother's face.

"I used to live here," she said. "As a matter of fact, you were conceived in that room right there," pointing to the window of the bedroom.

"Ew! Too much information, Mama..."

"PG-13, maybe. I'll never share the rest. At least, with anyone but him."

Clomp! Clomp! Clomp!

"There you are! It's about time. Why didn't you write? I didn't know where to find you," Grandma said, her arms open, her cane clutched in one hand, as she waited for a hug.

"Grandma? You don't look a day older than when

I…um…left," she stuttered, then got lost in the hug.

Grandma held her tight, not wanting to let her go lest Alexandra leave her world again. "I may not look older," she whispered, "but now I really do need the cane."

"I'm sorry I didn't write. I didn't know your address…"

X knew how lame her answer was, and Grandma called her out on it. "All you had to do was write Krista Rachmaninoff, Barrow, Alaska on the envelope and it would have come right to me."

"Honestly, if I hadn't been so hurt, I might have written…"

"Wait, just a second," young Krista said, her hand on both women's shoulders. "Excuse me for interrupting, but you're Krista, too?"

"Yup! Just like you. We're both Krista Rachmaninoffs. You were named after me!"

"Mo-om?"

"Yes, you were. At least, on your first birth certificate. When your daddy adopted you, we changed your name. Legally you're Krista Swenson, but you were brought into this world as Krista Alexandra Rachmaninoff."

"Wow! That's so cool! I'm going to change it as soon as

we get back home."

"Nope!" Grandma declared.

"Huh? Why not?" Krista asked.

"Change it today. Just claim it right now, in front of witnesses. The paperwork can come later. That's just the white man's busy work. You're half Inupiaq. We do things differently around here. At least we do every chance we get. This is a good opportunity."

"Okay, before everyone in this room, I declare that the name I want to be known by is the name I was born with: Krista Alexandra Rachmaninoff!"

"Here! Here!" Grandma and X cheered, then all three shared hugs and tears.

"Now, as I was saying," Grandma continued, wiping her eyes with one sleeve of her kuspuk, using the cuff of the other one to wipe under her nose. "I have a whole box of letters for you I was supposed to forward as soon as I had your address." She pointed to the pile in the corner, three sealed boxes, bulging at the sides, the tape on the bottom ones yellowed with age. "About twenty years worth. You can read them later. Right now, I just remembered that I forgot to tell you thank you for giving me a granddaughter. I thought you were his red raven, even when he called you 'not his girlfriend.'"

X put her hand up to pause Grandma when she heard her son's voice.

"Are you sure we shouldn't go to the hospital?" Lars asked, his voice coming from outside.

She frowned as she looked to the doorway, the screen door shut, the brightness outside making everyone inside hard to see for anyone coming into the house. There's no way Lars knew his mother and sister were here.

"I keep a spare medical kit here. It's closer. Besides, I don't charge when I fix you up away from the clinic. Let me clean up the scrape and put a bandage on it. I'm pretty sure you don't need stitches, but infections are my main concern."

X took two steps back and melded into the wall. After all these years, his voice had the same warmth and confidence, deep but not basso, the clipped rhythm of a Native Alaskan, the earthy tone that made her loins tingle, her stomach clench.

The door opened and Lars came in. "Have a seat at the kitchen table," Rocky said, then followed him in. "Hi, Grandma," he said. "Hi, guest," he added when he saw she

169

wasn't alone, nodded to the young red-haired woman, and proceeded to the kitchen and his new patient.

Grandma's mouth was open, ready to speak, but X caught her eye, shook her head, and put finger to lip, asking her wordlessly to be silent. Grandma nodded and complied, then toddled to her rocker and picked up her bag of crochet work.

X slumped to the floor and watched as Rocky tended to her son's scraped knee, his manner as gentle on a teenage boy as it was on a cut and scared young woman twenty-two years ago. "Now, this is going to feel cold. Watch my ears, not my hands, okay?"

"Yes, Doc," Lars said, then bit his lip in anticipation. Tired of watching his mender's ears, Lars looked around the room, then realized who the woman Doc had greeted was.

"Hey, Krista! What are you doing here?"

Krista grinned, not wanting to spoil her mother's surprise. "Oh, I was just in the neighborhood and heard this nice lady play the piano. Her name's Krista, like mine."

"Nope!" Grandma said. "Your name is Krista like *mine*. I'm older and had the name first."

"True," young Krista said, her grin widening as she tried

to control the rest of her comments.

"What's wrong?" Lars asked. "You're hiding something. I know you are. I've known you all my life and that smirk means you want to say something…"

"There. You're done, Lars. Keep it clean and no scrubbing floors or crawling on the ground for two weeks or until the scabs have fallen off, whichever comes first. And no picking at it!"

"Yes, Doc," Lars said, then stood up and looked toward where his sister had been sneaking sideways glances. "Krista, what's Mom doing, sitting on the floor?"

Rocky walked toward where Lars was looking, the slight creak of his metal ankle drawing her eye. X stared, glad she had been at least a little forewarned about the awesome basketball player with only one foot. She looked up at him and smiled nervously. "More than a couple pieces of broken glass, I take it?"

"X? Wha…What are you doing here?" he asked, reaching out to help her stand.

"Visiting with Grandma, watching you fix my son…"

Visions of family raced through Rocky's head, then he realized that X must have adopted a son, maybe even married. He smiled weakly. "Oh."

"You forgot to tell him we were witnessing the renaming of your daughter, too," Grandma said, nodding to Krista. "Tell him your name, sweetheart."

Krista bowed her head and blushed crimson, then took a deep breath, looked at him and declared, "I'm Krista Alexandra Rachmaninoff. Dad."

X and Lars rushed to Rocky, one on either side, supporting him as his knees buckled beneath him.

"Mom, he passed out. I mean, totally 'grab the smelling salts' passed out!" Lars said. "Cool! I thought that only happened in the movies."

"I guess it was too much of a shock to his system, huh?" Krista said. "Maybe I shouldn't have called him Dad."

Back from the kitchen, damp washcloth in hand, X lifted Rocky's head and placed the rag behind his neck. "Nah. He probably was already on his way down when you said your last name."

Rocky inhaled deeply, awake at the coolness on his skin and the sound of X's voice. "You're not messing with me, are you?" he asked, looking into X's face for signs of bedevilment. "She really is mine?"

"Ours," X answered. "One day of unrestrained passion was enough."

"Mo-om," Lars and Krista chorused.

"That's my grandson!" Grandma sang out. "If it's worth doing, it's worth doing right."

***

"So, what happened?" X asked, sipping her tea with him at the kitchen table. "The last I recall, you went to the store for milk and then, boom! You were gone forever."

"I didn't have the nerve to tell you that I had signed up for deferred enlistment into the army. The recruiter got me a plane ticket to Anchorage. I goofed up on the date, thinking we had another day before I had to leave. I was going to tell you that night, but I…um…kinda got sidetracked…" He glanced up at Krista, then lowered his eyes again.

"And…" X prompted.

"I had to leave or get thrown in jail. At least that's the lie the recruiter told me. By the time I found out what a fraud he was, it was too late. I'd already signed the final enlistment papers and was on my way to Fort Leonard Wood in

Missouri. I'd never felt such heat, but plugged away, basic training all day, write a letter to you each night and post it to Grandma's, then more training. I guess you never got the letters or reached out to see if Grandma knew where I was or what was going on."

"I'm sorry. It's as much my fault as yours. Or maybe more so. I had to deal with Dr. Jackass, then my mother, then I reconnected with my grandmother and found out I was pregnant..."

"And all alone?"

"No, I never felt 'all' alone. I had my grandmother and I had our child. I gave her your name, worked on my career in the health care industry..." X winked at Rocky and continued. "And then Karl came into our lives. He fell for Krista, then me, and then we were married. Six years and thousands of dollars of fertility specialists and procedures later, we had Lars. Karl died last year. So, here we are. When did you come back?"

"I thought you were going to ask about the foot first..."

X shrugged and said, "I figured it'd come up eventually. Whatever you want to tell me first is good with me. I didn't realize how much I missed your voice."

Low, guttural groans came from both Krista and Lars. X fixed them with a glare, then turned to Rocky and said, "You were saying…"

"I wound up in Afghanistan. Rough and cold in the winter and supposed to be absolute hell in the summer, but we didn't make it that long. I was an infantryman, a foot soldier, nothing special. We were on a scouting mission when the guy ahead of me stepped on an IED—improvised explosive device. Those hill people could make a bomb out of anything, even hand lotion…or so I've heard," he said, adding a wink.

X blushed at his silent 'kiss' and the fact he remembered she had complained that her lotion had been seized by airport security during the first conversation they had ever had in 1994.

"It killed the guy and didn't do me any good," Rocky pulled his pant leg up, showing his prothesis that started six inches below his knee. "I grabbed a tie down, wrapped it above the mess so I didn't bleed out, then crawled to help the others. I carried them on my back as I scooted across the rocks toward protection. You see," he turned to Lars, "the bad guys knew we were in their backyard and they were shooting at us."

"And with all the crawling in the dirt, you got an infection, huh?" Lars asked.

"Boy, howdy!" Rocky said, "but that came later. One of the guys radioed in for support while I shuttled in the last two."

"What about the others?" Krista asked. "Wasn't anyone else helping you?"

Rocky sighed and shook his head, holding back the tears as he relived the terror. "They tried, but they could stand up and run, so they did. They couldn't outrun a bullet, though. The explosion had separated us. We were two teams now. I saw the first men get taken down along with their buddies they were trying to help to safety. 'Get low!' I screamed, but it was too late for them. Or so I thought. I heard one of them moan. A few of the others had made it to a protected area and hollered they were going to wait for air support. 'Any minute,' they had told them, meaning the air support was on the way.

"Well, to me that meant it was even more important to get the man on the ground out of there. Long story short, I got him to safety, performed some first aid, and got him stabilized before the attack helos came in—the next day—

and neutralized the area, chasing the bad guys back further into the hills. They brought us in, shipped us to whichever specialty hospitals were deemed necessary, and that was that. Or so I thought.

"I knew I would be discharged early because of the injury. That was fine with me. I didn't know if you were finally getting my letters by this point or not. I wanted to come home. While I was in rehab, I found out that the letters were still accumulating," he nodded to the corner, "so I decided to change my focus. The last guy on the ground that I had pulled in had a rich family. He knew me by name and found me just before I was out of the system. His father wanted to thank me in person. We met up, he told me how special I was, that without my skills his son would have died, so he felt he owed me a debt. I think he wanted to buy me a car or something. I told him not to worry. I'd been mending folks since I was yay high," and held out his hand. 'Just in a day's work for me,' I said.

"Then let's do it with some letters after that long Russian name of yours. So, he paid my way through medical school. I'm now an M.D., believe it or not."

"And you work at the clinic?" X asked.

"As needed. I've sorta developed my own community outreach program."

"Basketball and bingo therapy?"

He answered her with a smile and a chuckle. Even after twenty-two years, they were thinking alike.

"Mom, can we move up here?" Lars asked, glad Doc and his mother had finally finished talking, even if it meant they were making googly eyes at each other.

She looked at Lars and said, "Just a sec. Rocky, let me see your watch."

He set his hand on the table and pulled off the band, the inside of his wrist to the table. She took his hand and turned it over, revealing the small tattoo M4L where the watch band had been. She took off her own watch, flipped her hand over, and showed him her tattoo, identical to his. "I traced over your ink for months, then finally went and had it made permanent. Looks like you did the same thing," she said, running her fingers over his pulse spot.

"Hurt like hell," Rocky said, "but it was pain for a moment, marking my devotion to my red raven, mated for life."

"Mom?" Lars asked. "You didn't answer me."

"Yes, Lars, we can finally move home."

"My years of hardships have passed, and my gray hairs have arrived," Rocky said, her hand in his.

"Your red raven is here, but she brought along a couple of chicks…"

"I'm not a chick, Mom," Lars said.

"And neither am I," Krista added.

"Bonuses," Rocky said.

X looked around the room. "It's gonna be a little snug in here, don't you think?"

"Nope." Rocky waited for all of them to get the identical puzzled looks on their faces. "The bedroom belongs to Joe and Grandma. Yes, they're still together. The living room is for the piano, courtesy of my saved wages from the U.S. Army, but I don't live here."

"Yeah… Are you going to show us or tell us?"

Rocky stood up, then put his arm around X to bring her to the front door. "See that two-story house over there on the rise? It's small but efficient."

"Three bedrooms?" Lars asked.

"Two," Rocky said, then turned to X and winked. "You get the couch, Lars. Builds character."

Chapter 11

The next day

"So, you're forty-three years old now, right?" Rocky asked, tracing her midline up from her navel to her throat, eager to ask but still as timid as a twelve-year-old asking for his first dance.

"Yes, but I don't think that's what you want to ask me, is it?" She brought his finger to her mouth and nibbled the end of it, teasing it with her tongue before placing it back at his side.

"No, not really…"

"My boobs got bigger when I nursed Krista and then stayed big—at least, up to average size—after I dried up. They got bigger still with Lars, but that might have been because it took so danged long to wean him."

"That's not what I was going to ask. And you know what you're doing to me, talking about nursing babies…"

X looked down, certain that he meant he was getting aroused again. "Well, I'll be…" then bent to his chest and decided to do a little suckling of her own.

Rocky arched his back. "What…what are you doing?"

Gently grasping his nipple between her front teeth, X mumbled, "Holding you hostage until you tell me what you really want to ask me."

"Well, if this is torture, you may never find out," he chuckled, squirming beneath her.

She let loose suddenly. "Okay, then. I won't do it again until you ask."

"Are you still fertile?" he blurted out.

She giggled in response. "What? You want more babies?"

He shifted to his side, his embarrassment gone now that the big question had been brought out. "Short answer, yes. Long answer, I missed so much, not seeing Krista grow up. I mean, she was the miracle that I never got to see. Shoot! I didn't even know about her until a day ago. I guess what I'm asking is, you wouldn't do anything…drastic…if you found out you were forty-three and pregnant, would you?"

"Uh? No! But whether it's in us to have another child or not, it doesn't mean we can't keep trying. Seems to keep Grandma and Joe happy."

"Do you think Krista will want to stay around here?" Rocky asked, his fingers tracing the old scars on her belly, watching to see how high her goose bumps would rise.

"If you're asking do you think she'd want to stick around and find a husband, then we could watch our grandchildren grow up in case we didn't have any more—well, only time will tell. When Oscar and Lisa showed up with their three to see if it was true that Red Raven had returned, I could swear Krista blushed when she saw Ivan. I doubt it was love at first sight, but I'm sure she had some immediate infatuation with the boy."

"With the man," Rocky corrected. "He's twenty-one and the same age we were when we first got together. And so is she. Whatever they find together is fine with me. As long as they keep the lines of communication between them open. I'm still more sorry than you can imagine that I didn't tell you what was going on before it was too late…"

X put her hand up, her fingers gentle on his lips. "No sorrier than I am. Please, let's not ever bring that up again, all right?"

He opened his mouth and wrapped his lips around her fingers, then tickled the tips of them with his tongue briefly before taking her hand away, kissing the back of it and putting it on his chest. "Now where were we..."

"I think we were talking about long odds and hoping Oscar and Lisa and crew were going to distract Lars and Krista for at least another hour."

"An hour? You're not getting off that easy, Mrs. Rachmaninoff. I have a lot of years to make up."

X bent to his chest, mumbled, "Me, too," then latched on, happy to have found a way to drive him crazy, too.

**

One year later

Ivan held one hand while his other one supported Krista's back. "She said just one more push," he translated. "You're strong. I know you can do it. The first one's always the toughest."

"Huh? First one... OW!

"Breathe... Huff, huff..." Ivan watched the midwife nod once, letting him know it was time again. "Okay, let's bring him or her into the world to meet everyone."

Krista took a deep breath, glad her husband and father literally had her back, then bent forward, praying that this would be the last push.

X, standing behind the midwife, said, "And here he comes…"

"Can I watch?" Rocky asked his daughter, ready to let go as her other back supporter.

Krista quickly nodded, still pushing. Now she knew that her mother was right. A woman's modesty did disappear in the delivery room. After all, he was watching his first grandchild come into the world, not looking at her naked bottom. It was also handy that he was a doctor, a backup. She trusted the old midwife who had delivered most of the babies in the region for the last forty years, but complications did arise. Hopefully, not today, though.

"Stop!" the midwife said in English, then quickly unwrapped the cord from around the babe's neck. "Okay. Again push."

"Ugh!"

"Save your breath for pushing," Rocky said. "The hard part is ov… Oh, wow."

Rocky's tears spilled over as he watched the midwife pull his grandson out the rest of the way, the white waxy vernix covering his purplish body making him look like an alien. But he wasn't. He was another native-born human, perfect in every way he could see.

The midwife set the baby on Krista's draped belly and grabbed the stainless steel bowl from the cart beside her. "One more poosh," she said, ready to catch the afterbirth.

"That one was easy," Krista puffed, then relaxed back into the pillows. Spent but ecstatic.

Ivan took the knife the midwife offered and cut the cord, beaming with pride. Flawless delivery. Flawless child. Flawless wife and marriage.

"May I?" Rocky asked, reaching for the baby. "It'll just take a minute."

Krista looked up at Ivan, making sure he agreed. "Go for it, Dad," Ivan said. "But make it quick."

Rocky did a rapid Apgar assessment of his grandson, wiped him down, then did a second test, confirming the first one. Perfect. He wrapped him snuggly in the soft flannel blanket then handed him to his daughter.

"It's best to try and get him to nurse right away," X said.

Krista wiped her teary eyes again and said, "I know, Mom. I've read every book in the library and on the internet and listened to you and Dad and everyone else in Utqiaġvik for the last nine months." Her breast now bared, she tickled her son's cheek with her nipple. He quickly turned his head and latched on. "Oh!"

"Yup. Perfect score," Rocky said. "Knows where his next meal is."

Lisa stuck her head in the door. "I'm not bugging you again about whether we can come in yet, but X, your son needs you. He won't be tricked by a finger and spits out the pacifier. He wants the real deal."

X looked down at her chest and realized she was leaking. Yup, she and her son were in sync—when he was empty, she was full.

"Let me have him. You and Oscar can come in and meet your new grandson."

"Grandson? We have a boy?" Oscar asked, his head peering over his wife's shoulder, hungry Louie Rachmaninoff squalling in his arms.

"I got a nephew?" Lars asked, trying to crowd in the doorway to get a look, too. "All right! A baby brother and a nephew! Two more members for the basketball team!"

"Here," Rocky said, approaching the door. "Let me get out so you three can come in to meet the latest resident of

Utqiaġvik, the northernmost city in North America."

"The coldest *and* the warmest place on earth!" X added.

"And happy to call it home."

THE END

A Note from the Author

Thanks for reading ONE ARCTIC SUMMER.

If you enjoyed the story, please help others know about what impelled you to finish it by reviewing and recommending it on Amazon and/or Goodreads.

To hear about new books and box sets in the works, please sign up for my newsletter and follow me on BookBub and Amazon.

Other books by Dani Haviland

<u>A Stingray Christmas</u>: (First book in the Arlie Undercover series) Anchorage detective on medical leave travels from Alaska to Arizona to see for the first time the son he'd fathered as an anonymous sperm donor. Great and rotten surprises await the cop with the smartest smartphone around.

<u>The Biggest Heart Ever</u>: (Book two in the Arlie Undercover series) When would Arlie learn that trying to do everything by himself could be deadly—and make Charlene a widow before they were married?

<u>Always a Bigger Fish</u>: (Book three in the Arlie Undercover series) Back in Alaska, Arlie finds out he's a target. Will vacationing detective Billy Burke (from THE FAIRIES SAGA) have information to help nab the scalper?

THE FAIRIES SAGA SERIES (in order with novellas):

<u>Naked in the Winter Wind</u>: (lengthy novel) How does an older woman wind up as a young hottie in Revolutionary War era North Carolina? First book in the time travel series.

Ha'Penny Jenny: (historical novella) More about the naïve and psychic young girl who was adopted into a time traveling family. Will her past catch up to her?

Aye, I am a Fairy: (lengthy novel) Young British lord finds himself entwined with a time traveling family and must decide if he should go back in time, too. Second book in the series.

Dances Naked: (novel) Directionally challenged time traveler is rescued by Cherokee in 18th century. What must he do before the chief will show him to The Trees, the portal through time?

Chasing Christmas: (historical novella) A young Cherokee is rescued from an abusive man and changes the lives of many in this 18th century America family.

The Great Big Fairy: (lengthy novel) Very tall Benji grew up in the 20th century but was born in the 18th. When he finds a way to return to his grandparents in the distant past, he goes for it. Once there, he realizes he can't stay, but must return to the future. Fourth book in the series.

Little Bear and the Ladies: (historical novella) What's a bachelor trapper to do with all the females he rescues from the Hessian mercenaries? He'd better hurry and figure something!

Little Drummer Boy: (historical novella) Young Scout works to earn money for a home in post-Revolutionary War America but runs up against prejudices and snowstorms.

Never Too Young: (historical novella) Scout and Ha'Penny Jenny have grown up, but will they be able to spend their life together, or will the past and ruffians get in their way?

Time in a Little Blue Bottle: (time travel 'mash up' novella) Elvis, Mark Twain, and the prime vampire are racing to get the bottle of Fountain of Youth water before sweet Bella and the youthful pickpocket. So why are time travelers Marty Melbourne and Master Simon interested?

CONTEMPORARY NOVELLAS – BENJI, THE LOST YEARS

Luke the Unexpected: Love of classic motorcycles brought them together, but Luke and Holly have other challenges to face. Find out how their friend Benji got his stripes here.

Pool Boy Wanted: No Experience Preferred (rather racy) Young Benji has been a hostage and slave, but life gets worse when an older woman decides she wants him as her own.

STAND ALONE NOVELLA

<u>Kit Kringle: An Alaskan Tale:</u> (contemporary) Kay moved to Alaska for the wrong reasons, then decided to stay and start her own business. What she hadn't planned on were prejudices and falling in love.

<u>Be My Angel</u>: Wyatt's dream to help save the wild mustangs began with the purchase of a rundown ranch in western Oregon. What he hadn't anticipated was being mesmerized by a sassy woman in a wheelchair.

<u>Three Are One</u>: The post chaplain tried to help the young widow adjust, but would his feelings for her and the search for his lost sister cause problems?

 Dani Haviland has never been one to believe, "You can't do that!" She started her own business in 1994, selling tractor parts in Alaska, then segued to writing and publishing books, becoming a USA Today bestselling author in the process. She currently splits her time between Alaska and Oregon, tirelessly writing and gardening, publishing and promoting, while claiming to be 'retired.'

Contact:

Dani Haviland can be found at:

www.danihaviland.com

Twitter: @dani_haviland

Facebooks: Dani Haviland Author

Email: dani@danihaviland.com